中夜

AWishBright Entertainment

© 2016 by Po Wah Lam

Take the night train. Take the sun, the dog, the friend. Take them and fly

To
Joyce
Jenny
Josie
Chloe
Sienna
Zosia
Kathy
Becky
Britt
Amali
Maiko
Tongtong
The Cat
and to
Graham
for granting life at the playground

On the wall of the bell tower the
symbols say: "Above and to your left
is a room," but there is no room

BOOK I

The Forgotten Station

I REMEMBER the day I found the key. It was the same day I returned to the island. At first I did not remember anything. The ferry blew its horn and left me standing at the water front. There I took a photo of the shops and the tall bridge above the shops that was as long as the island itself, all very shiny and bright.

I was looking for my grandparents, but did not know where they lived. So the first thing I did was to ask someone and that someone turned out to be adventure.

She was sat under a tree next to a cart full of steaming *jookjha*, meaning: sugar cane.

I walked up and said, "Hello," Slowly she looked at me and my suitcase.

"How much?" I asked.

"Tuppence," she replied.

This satisfied me and so I gave her what she wanted in return for what I wanted. But what I really wanted was to find my grandparents.

"They make beancurd," I said, "Do you know them?"

She shook her head and gave me the stick wrapped in paper. "Nobody does that anymore. But I suppose you could try the south end of the island."

"South?"

"Yes," she said, "Over there," and pointed past the mountain of trees on my right.

I looked. "Thank you," I said.

Not long after this I found a stone trail and was going steadily uphill. This was good because I remember a stone trail was the way to my grandparent's house. The not so good was my suitcase. It was quite heavy and slowed me down. I therefore took many breaks, sitting on the case while trying to enjoy the views. I did not see much at first. Most of it being trees and the odd closed gate with no house behind it, and when there was a house nobody lived in it. Nevertheless I kept walking until I came to something even more scary, a cemetery.

It was here that I changed my mind and turned back. The trail appeared to cut through the cemetery and then up a pass, which meant there was still probably a long way to go. Also I did not like the bones I saw. It was not far from the graves and it looked like the remains of a dog that had been tied to a tree and left to die.

This got me very upset thinking how it must have suffered being unable to get away. I ran from the place crying. It was good that I did because I would not have met Wando the dog who was to make me happy again.

She was standing behind a closed gate while I was sat in front of the gate, on my suitcase. I was startled at first. A dog! But this one was alive and standing behind me as if from out of nowhere, but this quickly changed to good news because suddenly I did not feel so alone or sad or afraid.

"Hey..." I muttered. I wiped my eyes and turned myself around.

There was no answer. The winds hummed. But I was certain it needed help for when it sat down on its haunches watching me I could see there was a wound on its front leg. A sad pair of eyes that kept looking at me, that seemed to say, *Please help!* I drew in for a closer look.

"Does that hurt? Would you like me to look at it?"

Again, it just looked at me.

"I am looking for my grandparents. Do you know them?"

I looked past the gate hoping I might get an answer. But all I could see were leaves and vines blocking what looked like a ruined tower. It was then that a strange feeling suddenly came over me, as if I had been here before.

I stood back. I looked at the mail box. There were letters sticking out. I read the address: "15A The Peak, Flower Flats". I could tell that no one had touched them for a long time because the paper was worn and crinkled and the post mark was months, if not years old.

"Looks like you live alone. That's so sad!"

I tried the gate but it was locked.

"You are locked in too?"
I did not think there would be a key but after seeing the dead dog, the thought of this one all alone, hurt and hungry made me feel uneasy and I looked hard for ways to open it. Finally I tried to climb over the fence and that was how I found it, the key!
The key was very big and I was surprised how big it was. I found it hanging behind the wooden support which held up the roof of the gate. The gate itself was built like a hut and quite old. It felt very exciting to find a secret key. And even more exciting when I turned the key inside the keyhole and it worked.

"I will just have a quick peek," I promised myself. "And then I will leave."

The gate did not make much noise but the leaves under me crunched like egg shells. But before I could get close the dog was gone. Suddenly it had vanished. And before me was a path curving away like a green tunnel, with leaves that were low and prickly. "It wants me to follow," I said to myself. And this I quickly did. I kept my head low most of the way but could not avoid the thorns tearing at my skirt. It felt like forever but at last I came to an opening. It was here, a drop below my feet, that I saw steel tracks hidden behind tall grass.

I gasped. It was a railway! I was now standing on a platform!

This, I would later come to understand belonged to the abandoned station which, when it closed was turned into a *miew*, meaning a nunnery or holy place. And beyond this was a cliff of sorts with many trees and there, was where I found her.

She was sat just beyond the archway, with her back to me and facing the sea. And on her back was the strange wooden sword.

She kept her distance at first. But later, whenever I got up close she would begin to sniff me.

Around the island she was known as Wanda or Wando, which means "found it". Wando was to become my best friend. And that summer on Joan Island, an island named after a saint which was where my grandparents lived was the best summer and one I still wish I did not have to leave. This place up the hill where no one wanted to live.

Joan Island is not really an island. Once there were trains that ran twice every hour linking it to the mainland. These trains came through a long dark tunnel which at that time was the longest tunnel in the world. But the trains have long gone, and its tracks and stations have long since vanished under tall trees and tall tales.

Today no one goes there and the only thing that lives at the station next to the mouth of the great tunnel are strange noises, angry spirits and, a dog. A dog that liked to bark down at the tunnel thinking its own voice is another dog on the other side. But was there?

That day I stood there for sometime watching her not knowing I was. She was a strange thing. Haunting a strange place. A dog not too big and not too small, with gold coat, sad eyes and sharp pointy ears that is fairly common for this part of the world. But her attention was fully captured elsewhere. Perhaps it was the sound of the waves below which, if you stood close to the mouth of the arch can sometimes sound like church bells.

When at last I stood at the spot where she sat it was very clear to me that this dog was a loner and, that I knew this place for I felt certain I had been here before. It was probably because of this that I decided there and then to stay the night under the arch. It was getting dark and I felt someone had to take care of her. And vice versa, someone to take care of me.

Dogs are not like horses. They are not beast of burden but this one carried something very strange, a wooden sword. At first I wanted to laugh. But the thing was painted white. "This is talisman," I said to myself. "It is meant to protect her." And because of this, and the feeling I had been here before that I did not feel so afraid about spending the night at the abandoned train station up the lonely hill.

The first thing I did was to try and offer it some food. I had a sandwich left over from my flight and so I tried that. She took her time, but finally walked over and took it.

"This is such a sad, sad place," I said, looking around myself. "You poor thing!" And at this, she raised her swollen face and looked up. A face badly bitten by insects. "But not to worry. Soon we'll make it happy!"

The Scouts handbook always taught us to be prepared and this I pleasantly was. From my suitcase I took out a first aid kit and began carefully cleaning her wound. She did not say anything as I did this and seemed happy for me to put on a big plaster. I then took out a pile of dried leaves. With this I struck a match. The leaves burned, giving off pleasant odour which quickly swirled around us.

"There!" I said, feeling better myself. "How does that feel? Better? No more pain and bites and no more hunger!"

That was how I felt about things, then. And the reason why I had to get passed the gate and trespass, which was the only time I have ever done anything bad in my whole life. As a girl scout I was not happy about this, but since I was still in uniform, in a strange way I was happy.

I walked over to the big station sign. It was hidden behind tall grass and was made of wood. The red paint was peeling away around it but at its center the word was still very clear. It was the word "Jung" or "Joan" which means: centre or middle.

"My name is Joan," I said to myself.
"And this is Joan station on Joan
Island. I have nothing to fear!"

Quickly I set about looking for
pools and puddles, anything that
might have held stagnant water. There
were many empty flower pots and
puddles on the platform to which I
wasted no time in getting rid of.
This I knew would also stop biting
insects from returning.

It felt good to keep the insects and
hunger away but there were other
things unseen which I could not keep
away.

"So you really do live all alone," I
said, looking back through the
archway. And though I did not really
believe in ghosts, I held back from
saying what I thought. Instead I
cautiously scanned the place as if
worried I might find someone or
something telling me to get out.

There were many things there, on the
platform facing the sea. The one I
liked best was the old platform
clock. It did not hang but stood on a
post, which I could see stopped
somewhere past midnight. The old
bench was also good. I found a lamp
there. I picked it up. It was broke
and had no paraffin. There was even a
broom (which I used) and a dented
spyglass (which I also used). With

this I looked down at the beach and across the ocean where I saw a ship and a plane slowly moving away. I then walked around the whole building looking through all the windows making certain that no one was home. Satisfied, I then checked the lonely bell tower, the one I could see from outside the gate. It stood on its own at the back, near the cliff. The door was locked yet I did not see a lock. Strange symbols and holes were carved into the high wall and I tried to read them as the sea of trees whispered around me.

But above all else, what I really wished to see was the spooky old tunnel. For this was the most mysterious looking thing of them all. It hid behind a veil of leaves and all you could see was a dark slit where the railway disappeared into.

It was not that far from the platform and soon, after crossing a stream I plucked up the courage to find out what was behind this dark, leafy gap.

It was an even bigger and darker
gap, like a mouth. A great, big
opened stone mouth that seemed to
have eyes for above it, one on each
side rose small towers with a single
window. But this big mouth was now
shut. wooden planks and beams had
been pushed up against it for so long
that they have rotted, especially
near the bottom, which made the mouth
look like it had jaws.

"I wonder where this goes?" I
muttered, as I stood there listening.
It sounded like another sea, with

gulls calling far away on the other side. But something closer was just as hollow. At the entrance, like two chimneys stood large hollowed out stones. They looked like chimneys but I knew they could not be. Perhaps they were a kind of door spirit which every house on the island must have to protect it from evil. Except these were the other way round, meaning it prevented evil from coming out.

Suddenly I felt a presence standing next to me. I turned and gasped.

"Oh! It's you!"

She walked forward and raised a front leg, the leg that was wounded. Then she looked back at me, waiting as if she wanted me to follow, as if she could see something through the cracks which I could not.

"Come now. There is nothing there. Let's go down to the beach!"

It was getting dark but as I have said, having this dog and sword made me feel strangely secure. Many stone steps led down to the beach and when we got there I found it sandy and smooth. And because the tide was out we saw many sand bubbler crabs. We followed their balls going so far out that when I looked back, I saw the tower and the island had turned black against the sky.

I knew I had to be very careful now.
The island had many green snakes
which are poisonous. I found one when
I went back across the tracks to
fetch my suitcase. One moment the
track was empty and the next, a green
coil was there. Its eyes were blood
red and it lay still as a rock. How
it had got there so quickly scared
me. After this I always checked below
my feet, especially when turning
around.

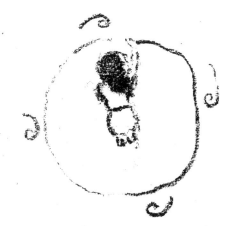

From my suitcase I took out a piece
of chalk and drew a large white
circle under the arch, the spot I
intended to sleep that night. I then
took out a hammock and insect net to
go over the hammock. I strung it up
just before it got dark and gathered
firewood to cook my supper. I could
have cooked with running water from
the stream but I found a tap. It

faced the sea and held a small sink under it. At first it was frightening because it spluttered very loud. The neck choked back and forth as if it was alive. When finally water came it was very muddy.

I did not like this noise it made and so turned it off as soon as the water was clear. While the rice was being cooked I heard another scary sound. It seemed to be coming from across the platform. *Tap, tap, tap* followed by another *tap, tap, tap*.

Quickly I finished off the protective circle I drew by putting in special words and symbols meant to keep away all things bad and evil.

I then said to the dog, "Stay inside this circle? Understand? We will be safe here." I was not sure if she understood but her nose did twitch to the smell of my cooking which to me was satisfactory enough.

That night we shared a tin of meat and vegetables with the rice. After that I was so tired I did not think anymore of the dead dog and neither did I care about the strange noises that echoed around us. I slept feeling a train might come roaring out of the tunnel.

2

IN THE MORNING I woke to the sound of birds. The sun soon rose and it was the most beautiful morning ever.

I opened my eyes and the first thing I looked for was the dog. I peered down from my hammock.

"Good morning," I said. My new friend raised her neck and looked up. She smiled and I smiled back. I climbed down and went to my suitcase. I got out my toothbrush and began brushing my teeth.

"What a lovely day! Did you sleep well? Are you hungry? How about breakfast? We could go down to the water front..."

The sun was behind us, beginning to push its rays through the arch. I looked down past the trees and onto the beach and then back again. Again it was the same stare. A big wondering stare as the sun glowed from behind the big pointing ears.

"I had a funny dream. I climbed a tree in that graveyard and could not get down. I did not want to get down. I felt scared but you came to my rescue. You are pacing round and round the bottom of the tree. I thought it was you. But it couldn't have been. This dog was big. You are not big. Are you?"

I wished to record the sound of morning and take pictures and both of these I did. From my suitcase I took out a tape recorder. I turned it on. I then took out my camera. I clicked and waited for the photo to slide out from under the camera.

The place looked very different now. The tide was in and the beach was small. Everything was so much clearer, especially the fruits high in the trees which were not very big. One tree I could see had pears on its branches as well as plums.

Once again I picked up the old broom. I went through the arch and began sweeping the other two platforms. Both were thick with leaves and sometimes sedges which needed pulling up by hand. But there were also broken snail shells which I think is the reason why there was so much crunching under my feet. I put the leaves into two large piles. Then, with a leaky wheel barrow I found and probably the best find of the day, emptied everything over the leafy edge down to the beach.

While I was sat resting I heard the same *tap, tap, tap* I heard the night before. It was not as scary now in the daylight but still I felt fearful. I looked to my left and to my right. The only moving thing I could see was at the other side of the platform. A bird was pecking at something.

When it flew off I walked over to look. What I found made me smile. They were broken snail shells!

"So this is what the sound was..." I said to myself. "A bird pecking at snail shells!"

It was good to know what had me scared was so simple yet not everything was the same.

A large canopy of leaves surrounded the station and an even larger undergrowth of brambles and sedges.

I could not understand why this bramble had been pushed back, as if something had pushed it back. And because the brambles were kept at bay there grew wild flowers. At first I thought they were just flowers but when I brushed aside the leaves I found cucumber. I was surprised. There was food growing wild!

Pandanus, guava, agave, these grew all over the island by themselves but not cucumber. Perhaps these are special, I mused, smiling to myself. Because growing over and around them was more jungle than garden. I did not pick the cucumber but I did pick something else. Agave is tidy and is food but it also gives you a needle and thread. I cut one and pulled it out with its thread attached and placed it inside my neck purse for future use.

Today was day two and I was determined to find my grandparents. With the old basket I found by the bench I locked the gate and left the key back where it was and steadily made my way down to the water front.

I did not see the dog follow me but not long after it appeared.

"Where did you come from?"

She did not answer me but I knew she must know a way in and out that I did not. She stayed in front of me most of the way, stopping to sniff at flowers or to look at things I could not see. She seemed to know where I was going. But what I did not know at the time was that this was what she once did. Seeing pilgrims off and walking them down to the ferry.

It was still early and parts of the market had yet to open. I did not remember any of the streets or the shops. But as we wandered and waited for them to open, I took more photos and thought about me and my grandparents and how really, I was no stranger here. I also worked out I had enough money to live for a month but after that I would have to start fishing.

Later when my basket was full I bought some fish balls. This is a very popular snack and I gave the dog three on the spot which she found very tasty and returned to the old station thinking about the many people who stared at me and the dog walking at my side.

Not long after this, as if a show of
trust she began showing me the beach
and the places where she spent time.
The beach below us was fairly rocky
with many crevices and in them were
tide pools. This meant there was
probably a good chance that many
things lived there and there was. I
found starfish, anemones, crabs,
squid and sometimes, even cuttlefish.
These fun, lonely but "living" places
I could tell, were the places she was
willing to go and wanted me to
follow. But I was not willing to

follow or go into the "not living" places such as the dark railway tunnel or the old graveyard which was the only place I did not take any photographs of.

"I am not going in there!" I would say when passing. And yet Wando liked to put both her feet against the low wall and peer over, twitching her nose as if there was something living there which I knew was not. But this graveyard was strange. I had never seen one like this before. Each gravestone had a picture of the dead finely carved into it so that when the dim shadow of leaves fell across them it looked as if there were people staring out of a window, which made it even more scary.

I never saw her go into the graveyard because I always called her away but I know she went into the tunnel because I saw her go in.

Near sundown I heard a dog's bark. When I went over to investigate, I watched her push aside a plank and disappear.

"*Dog!*" I cried, for I did not know her name. "*Dog!*" I waited. But heard only the return of my own voice followed by a loud, bone-like *CRACK!*

"*Dog?*" I cried again. "Please come back!" It was then that I tried whistling for I knew dogs understand this better. I put my fingers to my mouth and blew. I whistled many times.

Finally after some moments I watched her return from the black hole, crawling back out through the broken plank.

"You scared me," I said. "Please don't do that again."

This tunnel was like a great hungry mouth. It swallows everything. Sunlight, sound and even memory if you let it. I feared Dog will go in one day and forget and never return.

And just to make certain she did not, I sealed off the gap by pushing many rocks and timber against it till I was sure she would go in no more.

"There! Now. I think it's time you had a wash. I think you need one. Agreed?"

I stood her by the tap. I took off the straw harness holding the sword and began rinsing her with soapy water. I washed off the salt and the sea knowing well the next day she would go and splash in the sea again then smell bad. Still, I scrubbed her clean until I was satisfied.

I then walked over the platform and stood on the old tracks. Abandoned railways do not shine like used ones. The steel is coated in rust and is brown. Only used railways shine because trains run on them wearing away the rust.

I stood there with the spyglass and looked far down the tracks both ways, first to where the sun was going down in the west and then east to where the black, hungry tunnel was, knowing that no matter how long I looked a train would never come. All the same I knelt down and touch the metal. It was hot. But more than that. I kept my hand on it and felt it throb as if it were alive and running. I did this often in the days to come and always I would stand up feeling certain a train was on its way.

Before going to sleep I left some water boiling on the embers so I could carry and drink on my third day. My third day again, began very early for I wanted to explore the rest of the island.

The island seemed to be divided into three parts. The low coastal parts was were most of the islanders preferred to live, with the mid hilly parts now and again lived in, but there were almost no one living high on the hills. It was sad and scary to see so many empty houses. Sad, because they looked to be nice places to live in. And scary, because the doors in all of these dead houses were wide open as if they were inviting you to come in.

"They must have been grand houses," I said to Wando. Perhaps they were churches because of the shape of the windows. So much of it had crumbled away that stone arches would appear alone in mid space, without the walls that once would have stood beside it which made it look very strange and out of place.

It was very much the same all over the island: hot and quiet.

To the east, over the hill and passed the graveyard lay the other side of the island. Here, I found no shops and few people and it was probably because of this that Wando came along. It felt good to have her at my side and I wondered whether this was another of her hang outs.

3

IT WAS SUSAN, the first person I spoke to on my first day of return. She told me that it was. I took a photograph of her as she came my way. When at last she came up close I showed her this photo and she looked pleased.

"I waited for you", she said. "You had me worried. Did you find your grandparents?

"No."

"What does your grandparent's house look like?"

"It was big," I answered.

"Anything else?"

"It was by the sea."

"Many houses are by the sea."

"There was a fruit tree,"

"That too,"

"And a black notice board."

"Black notice board?"

"Yes. I think it was made out of metal."

"Well, that's easy. It's in the south. It's the only black one I know on the island. Come. I will take you."

This day again was beastly hot. We followed the coast most of the way and the mountain, which was always to our left. It was as we walked that she began looking at the dog walking at my side.

"I see you have a friend,"

I nodded, smiling proudly.

"Her name is Wando. She lives up at the abandoned train station."

I pretended I didn't know and said nothing, pointing only to the sword which I was very curious about.

"Oh that. I think it repels evil. You see, when the station was still open Wando often walked visitors back down to the water front. That was her job, you see. Making sure the guests were safely on their way. We rarely see her nowadays. Ever since the last nun died there have been no more pilgrims and so no one to walk down to the ferry. I think it is a kind of talisman. It brings her good luck."

"I think so too."

"You do?"

I nodded again.

"I am Susan."

"I am Joan," I answered.

She looked at me and I at her.

"Susan is a very pretty name," I said.

She looked at me again.

"Do you think so?"

"Yes," I answered.

"Thank you," she said. She smiled at me and I smiled back.

There were many things I liked about Susan and Joan island. Cars being one. There were none. I did not see any cars nor motorbikes. The island was quiet most of the time with no noisy sea birds. I also liked the old people because they collected the cans and rubbish others did not want and were always busy. But Susan I especially liked. Not because she was the first person I spoke to on the island and that she helped me in many things. It was her understanding of flowers. "We make tea from this flower," she said. "Joan Island is hot but drink this and you will feel cool and strong."

I looked and smiled wide. She felt to me like a big sister.

What I did not like about the island was the poor, mucky animals tied to walls and gates and whose sad, angry barks are really their way of saying:

Hey! I want to be free, like you!

"Are those your dogs?" I said to one man. "How would you like it if you were tied up like that! With no place to run and no water to wash yourself?"

The man, who looked at me with fierce eyes told me to go away and I had to, because Susan said I should.

"That was Sawback, the Lock Man," she said. "Did you see his keys? He owns the most houses on the island, even the empty ones. His family is one of the oldest on the island. This means they have an ancient right to take a property if no one comes to claim it within a space of ten years."

"Does that include animals too?"

"Yes."

"But this is so sad and cruel," I said. By this I was of course remembering the bones I saw. The ones back up the hill with the rope still tied around its neck. This I told Susan which also made her sad but in the end all she had to say was,

"Never mind."

We passed another chained dog and I said the same thing and this man also told me to go away.

"You are a funny girl," Susan said afterwards, and placed her hand over my head. "But one day you will understand."

Perhaps it was because I did not understand that I took a photograph of that first dog tied to the wall with nowhere to go, which also made the man with the keys even more angry.

The black notice board was made of steel just as I remembered it. By the time we reached it the thing was quite hot under the sun. We stood there and looked at the houses leading from it.

"Perhaps behind one of these doors live your grandparents," Susan said. But no matter how many different doors we knocked on there was no sign of my grandparents or anyone who made bean curd.

"Nevermind," Susan said again, looking glumly down at me. "Perhaps we should go and have ourselves an ice bean. Would you like that?"

Ice bean is ice lolly made out of red beans.

"Yes please!" I answered.

We sat down with our ice beans while looking across the sea. It was there that Susan took my hand and with those big glasses she wore, read my future, which was something her grandmother taught her.

"What does it say?" I asked.

"It says," she said, answering slowly. "You will find your grand-parents."

I laughed and so did Susan. I then asked if she would read Wando's future and she did. But as the sun came down over the sea I did not get an answer and neither did I find my grandparents.

"I'll see you tomorrow," she said.

But tomorrow it rained, and the day after. So I did not see Susan at the place of sugar cane or found out whether her predictions came true. Instead I spent those rainy days at the station under the arch watching the rain fall.

I was glad to have this arch for shelter, which was always dry and made the bird songs sound so much richer. I searched every gap of that archway hoping I might, like the front gate, find a key. But I never did. There were two doors under the arch, halfway in. One led into the waiting room and the other, the ticket office. There was not much to see in the waiting room because of the partitions so that visitors could stay the night but at the ticket office, there were still stamping machines big and small next to a chair that looked like a station cat might have once slept there.

I did once find a key, but it did not fit any of the doors.

I spent much of this time making cords from the many sedges that grew around the station. I would put two pieces together and roll them across my knee to make one strong cord which I used for difference purposes such as: repairs to the old basket.

Sometimes Wando would turn from the rains and look at what I was doing. And other times it was me who looked up from my cord making to see a dog with a toy weapon. Animals are fun to watch anyway, especially one that carried a wooden sword and I always wondered about that. Who gave it her and why? "What a strange thing you are," I said. "Strange and mysterious. Like the night. If only you could talk. I'd be happy to hear stories about the station. The nuns and of all the things that have happened here."

But she could not talk and I wondered. And watched.

The rains washed down everything, leaves, sticks, spider webs, snail shells and even dragonflies that were clinging on the leaves and sedges.

I wished the rain could have washed down the call of frogs. I liked frogs for they ate the biting insects but not for the noise they were making. We often went down to the beach to look at the rock pools, thinking the rains might have brought out more fish but we hardly saw anything. Once I found an empty glass bottle. I took it back to the station and cleaned it. I then put inside it a message. I wrote:

"Help! Looking for grandparents! Have not seen them since I was three! Now I am 9! Staying at the forgotten train station up the hill with Wando the dog. It's a wonderful place. A bit creepy, but safe. If you know my grandparents, please tell them I am here. I am waiting. Yours faithfully, Joan at Joan island."

41

I pushed a cork into the top then slung it far out, to where the tides ebbed across a gloomy sea.

I did not take any photos in the rain. It was too gloomy. But I did take one. It was a picture of the flood. There was so much rain that the stream had become a river, tearing noisily down the mountain and onto the tracks. It was scary in a way, having the tracks under water and not being able to see them. It was like having a raging swimming pool in front of us. At one point the water rose so high it almost reached the platform. This scared me and I was set on climbing onto the roof for I was certain it would have swept us away. And yet when I looked at Wando, at how she looked calmly at the white water while sitting on all fours, I changed my mind.

"You have seen this all before. Right?"

The flood did not last long. Soon we were able to see the tracks again but by that time Wando was once again outside the tunnel. Even though she could no longer go inside because I had sealed it off, she still stood outside it staring in. Once she got very wet going there and back and the sword slipped. It ended up hanging under her belly which made her walk more crab than dog.

I looked at her and she at me. Her face spiky and wet. I laughed. "*Oh, you poor thing!*"

I kept a fire going most of the time to keep things dry and, the insects away. I did try the wild cucumbers and found they tasted the same as the market ones, if not better. We were almost out of fire wood when at last the rain stopped. It stopped round about midnight. As I have said there were many strange noises at the station, sometimes even noises and vibrations that made you think a midnight train was about to pass through, but the noise that came after the rains was scary because everything was so quiet. I got down from my hammock and walked over. The sound was hollow, like footsteps and seemed to come from the belfry of the tower. Wando came too and I could feel her brush against my leg. We stood outside the tower with my torchlight pointing up. I listened. It sounded like a pair of wings on descent, which then sounded like footsteps coming down.

Quickly I ran back to my hammock. I stayed there, inside my protective circle and did not come out until dawn.

The morning was sunny and because it was, people returned. The ferry busied in many people who did not live on the island and made the water front and the shops look very busy.

Susan came too. She was back at the place I first saw her, by the cart load of brewing sugar cane. She was busy when I came to but I could tell she had been looking for me.

"Where did you spend the last few days?"

"The hotel," I answered.

She looked at me in a funny way. There being only one hotel on the whole island.

"I went to the hotel."

"You did?"

"Yes."

I said nothing.

"I have found your grandparents."

"You have?"

"Yes. There are three steel notice boards around the island. They all used to be black but two have since been painted white. That is why we could not find your grandparents. Their notice board is now white."

4

I HAD WITH ME one photograph of my grandparents. In it Grandfather wore a hat and had his arms folded. While Grandmother had black hair and wore an apron. It was taken in front of their house and the door was wide open.

The house Susan took me to also had a door that was wide open. And the women who lived there also had black hair and wore an apron. When I said, "Grandmother?" and showed her my photo, I was picked up like a doll.

She began to cry and so did Grandfather, except he was trying to hide it. Even Susan was crying a little, especially after my grand-parents thanked her with a gift of dried bean curd. I felt very happy. But later as the sun burned low across the ocean and Wando stood at the gate wanting to be let out, I was not so happy.

"Are you sure you won't stay?"

She looked at me briefly. But that was all.

She was willing to walk me to my grandparents. Willing to stay and eat and spend time behind the gate but she was not willing to stay the night.

I watched her hurry back up the hill and then passed the bend where the last street light shone as if something better awaited her at the lonely station on the lonely hill where nobody lived.

I did not sleep too well at my grandparents, even though the place was big and comfortable. The first thing I did the next day at breakfast was to go and ask Grandmother about the lonely station on top of the hill. I suppose it was the sight of breakfast: a bowl of white noodles and sauce that made me remember.

"*Poy…*" said Grandmother, which was how old people often talk around the island. "When I was a girl, mother told me about Bride's Cave. She said when they were digging they broke into a burial chamber. This is why it was called Black Cave, the hole that goes to the other side of the world. It was renamed Bride's Cave after a bride was killed there. We were warned never to go in but how could we? A big dog lived there. It watched the hole day and night. It did not let anyone in except the trains, the Steel Beasts, we used to call them. When the trains stopped coming the station was lived in by nuns. It became a *miew*."

A *miew*, as I have said is a holy place. It's a word I liked because it sounds like a sweet cat. Now I knew why the station became a *miew* when it closed. It was to appease the spirits of Bride's Cave. To stop the bad things from coming into our world.

"Have I been there before, Grandmother? To this *miew*?"

"You have," she answered. "When you were last here, you spent many nights there. The tower was built by my sister, your Great Aunty Nign. You see those books?" She was pointing to some books inside a cupboard which I later would read. "They are hers. She and your uncle built many houses on the island. And all of us, your Grandfather and I and your mother have stayed and said our prayers in that place."

"Perhaps that is why I remember," I finally said. "A high place. A sky place, with pine trees and breakfast."

"That was the nuns. They must have got you breakfast. The *miew* was like a hotel and people stayed there. But it is closed now. No one lives there and no one goes there."

I did not tell her about my time at the *miew* and I never did. And neither did I take my suitcase from the station. After breakfast I went back to the station with some leftovers. I could tell Wando missed me because just as I neared the station, at the graveyard hill, we met. She was trotting over the hill looking for me the same way I was looking for her. I was so happy that I broke the silence of the graveyard by shouting "*Wando!*"

Nothing much had changed. Which I liked. The gate was still locked and the trains were still nowhere in sight. I turned on the noisy tap and washed my hands. I picked up the spyglass and spotted a faraway ship. The winds hummed. It was all the same as before but for one small thing.

I cupped her chin in my hands and looked. Below her left eye, at the nose bone was a deep, red mark like a knife cut. This I did not like.

Beancurd is first boiled and the skin that forms at the top is scooped out and allowed to dry. They look like cream coloured towels hanging out to dry. When they are dry it is packed and sold.

All morning I scooped out beancurd strips and all morning I kept wondering about Wando. Something must have attacked her. But what?

That night I told Grandmother I was staying over at Susan's place. I then returned to the mouth of Bride's Cave and looked. I looked because earlier that morning I had to go there and put more rocks against the hole.

After what Grandmother had told me about Bride's Cave I felt even more worried and wanted to make sure Wando stayed within my protective circle.

I knew something had come out. Something had pushed through and left behind tough hair and a large tooth. This tooth was bigger than my hand and heavy. It then went near the gate and made a big mess by eating nearly all the cucumbers and by digging great deep holes in the earth. It was this something I was certain, that attacked Wando who always wanted to make friends and would not fight back.

Perhaps it was because she did not know how to fight back that a sword was placed across her back.

I put another rock against the hole which I now carried from the beach. Then another, bigger one till I was satisfied. I was about to leave when I heard Wando bark. I turned around. Slowly I walked over and knelt down beside her, putting my hand over her back.

"What's there?" I asked. "What can you see that I cannot?" She did not look at me. Her mouth did not move. And neither did she bark.

But the sound came again. I looked. A chill ran down my spine.

The hole was barking!

5

AFTER THE RAINS there came many days when it was very hot. It was so hot that even the sand bubbler crabs stayed in their holes. We did not see them make their many balls.

It was probably because it was so hot that things died. It was early in the morning. I was on my way down to the water front when she picked up a dead bird I did not see. At first I tried to take it from her, thinking she would eat it.

"No!" I cried. But she ran from me and I could not keep up. When at last I got back up the hill she was digging. She had laid the bird down near the graveyard and was digging hard with both paws. I could see the bird now. It was light green and had a sharp beak. Too beautiful, I thought, to have died.

Since she was not going to eat the bird I let it be.

I watched her carefully lift the bird, putting it inside the hole which she then covered over by pushing back the earth with her snout.

when she finished I brushed the mud from her face.

I cried and said, "Good girl. You are a very good girl!"

Even though I knew that she had buried the bird like a bone, I still felt what she had done was special. As if she loved the bird and had laid it to rest. She would find and bury many more birds before the summer was over and many after but it was the fish. The fish impressed me the most.

There was something funny about the crabs and the balls they made. All that hard work only to have the tides erase them again. Wando liked the crabs too but as I have said, she much preferred the tide pools and this was where I found her late in the day. She was not on the platform as usual and so I went down to the beach to look. There I saw her come up with something in her mouth. It was a small fish.

But this one looked dead. It did not struggle. Again she wanted to play chase and would not let me get close. She ran with the fish to where the tide was coming in. What she did next made me very happy and surprised. She put the fish down in the water and slowly began nudging it. She nudged and nudged till the thing was no longer on its side but up. I watched the tail flip and slowly it swam away.

Throughout the summer I watched her do this quite a number of times. Sometimes the fish lived and sometimes not. But always they were easy to catch and looked quite dead. It happened mostly on rainy days and sometimes very hot days when the rocks themselves were too hot to touch.

I never again tried to take anything from her but I was beginning to spend more time at Joan station than I was at my grandparents. I loved my grandparents but Wando was showing me a new world all the time. My grandparents could easily take care of themselves but I was not so sure about Wando.

Even though Bride's Cave was sealed off I was still afraid.

I asked Grandmother about voices in the dark and she laughed, saying, "At my age I hear many voices. I hear them in the night, calling me. Voices of my ancestors long gone. They ask me to go with them and one day I will. When I tire of making beancurd I will answer their calls."

I knew something was calling Wando. Something like Grandmother had said. A voice, "long gone". A voice that will lead Grandmother away the same way it might lead Wando away which I did not want and I told her so.

"I love you, Grandmother," I said, holding her wet hand. "Don't ever leave me!" But she only laughed and said I was silly.

"I will always be with you. As long as you don't forget Grandmother I will be at your side. Always."

This I was mildly glad to hear. Yet there were no such words to comfort me about Wando. I did not want Wando to be led away, ever. And yet what was strange is she wanted me to go with her. This I knew was impossible and yet in a strange way I felt excited as I was afraid.

"It must be awful to lose your voice," I said. "Now I know why you need to go. You want your voice back, don't you? You want to bark again. A dog with no bark is not a dog. I am sorry I did not understand before but I do now. That tunnel must be a terrible place. Stealing your voice like that. A terrible place..."

But more than anything I felt it was meant to be. Joan station and I are one. And because I felt that, I knew that I was meant to understand the mystery on the wall of the bell tower and in the end I think I did.

6

MANY TREES GREW around the station but there were two especially tall ones which I felt I had seen before. On gloomy days and even sunny days I would stand and look at them for a long time the same way Wando would stand and look at Bride's Cave for a long time. I do not know what a dog saw in a black tunnel but what I saw in the trees, I felt certain I knew. It was a far off place full of magic. I knew this from the moment I first sighted the old tower.

The first key was the one found by the gate. This allowed me into the station. The second key was Grandmother.

"Your Great Aunty built that tower," she said. "Those books are hers," And it was from one of these books I looked through that I found the answer to the symbols that were carved into the tower wall. "*There is a secret room*," it said, "*Up high and to your left...*"

The first time I translated the symbols I knew it had to be a joke. Up the wall, where square holes zigzag acting like steps inviting you to climb, was nothing, meaning empty space. It was the side of the building and nothing more.

Whatever it was, I did like my Auntie's sense of humour. If that is what it was. Since I could not go up the locked tower I decided to go down instead, to see if I could climb one of the trees. What I found, when I got down was that neither of them could be climbed. There being no branches at all at the base, only at the very top. But I did come across a fallen tree.

Its torn roots lain against one of the two trees which had also prevented it from sliding all the way down and onto the beach.

It was this that made me see and see back in time. Into the past when this fallen tree was still living and stood growing next to the bell tower. It grew up, slanting from the cliff and probably had its branches close to where the bell tower stood. This tree, was in all probability the "secret room" the symbols spoke of.

"If so," I said to myself, "what was in this room? Was there anything at all?"

I looked. But found nothing around the rotted remains. There was nothing in or around the broken stem of the dead tree.

But I did not give up so easily.
There was something about the two
trees. But what? They were like
dancing twins and even had branches
that looked the same, but I felt and
knew that was not the real reason why
I looked and stared. I thought about
this for a long time. I thought it
over while walking down the rusty old
tracks and then down at the beach,
especially where the crabs made their
patterns and finally it was there

among the many sands balls that I knew what I had to do.

I needed to make a bow and arrow and climb the tower. And from there, shoot out a rope to reach the tall branches and thus, climb one of the two trees. It would be daring and difficult and I could not do it alone.

"If only you had fingers and a thumb like mine," I said to Wando who again raised a front leg and was looking into Bride's Cave.

I knew I needed to go and see Susan and so one day, after making one bow and one arrow, I did.

The first thing she said to me was, "I saw your Grandmother."

"You did?"

"She asked me what we did on the days you stay over at my place. I said: fishing. Did I answer well?"

I looked. Slowly I nodded and smiled.

"I am ready to share my secret with you now," I said.

"Secret?"

"Will you come?"

"Where?"

"Up the hill. To the old train station."

"You mean: where no one lives?"

I again nodded.

"Please," I said. Putting my hands together as if begging.

"Do you mind if I come later?"

I looked. Stalks of cane were steaming from her cart, but not many were left so I knew she would not be long.

"You promise?"

Silence.

"I also need a rope. Do you have one?"

"A rope?"

"Please. A long one. For climbing."

"When I am done I will bring it to you."

"Promise?"

"I promise."

She kept her promise and at dusk came to the gate carrying a bundle of knotted rope not knowing that I had the key. I hid myself behind the gate and she stood with her back to it, looking down the path both ways thinking that that was where I would appear. She did not expect that a hand would reach out from behind her with a stick and tap her across the shoulder.

The result was that she jumped, almost in mid air, but not before letting off a loud, "*Ahhhhh!*"

I jumped too. The scream was loud enough to reach Bride's Cave.

Then in a low whisper which I did not know why she said, *"what are you doing there? How did you get in?"*

"with this," I answered, whispering the same way she was. I lifted the big key from my pocked, holding it up like a flower.

She stood wide eyed and mouth opened, but said nothing more.

"Come. Let me show you."

It was late in the day and the light was low. This was the best time to see the station with the light shining on the leaves and down into the archway.

"So this is where you stayed before we found your grandparents."

"I still do, sometimes." I said. *"why are you whispering?"*

She looked. *"So are you!"*

"I will stop if you will."

"Deal!"

We laughed and began talking normal again.

"You lost one point," I said.

"How come?"

"You screamed!"

It felt good to at last walk the platform together and have questions answered that a poor, lonely dog could not answer. At first we simply walked and looked at the many things around the platform. The gas lamps, the broken trolley, the big machine behind the ticket office which Susan said could be used to print your name on a metal tag.

But even though there were lots to see and lots to say, I could tell what Susan really wanted to see and say was Bride's Cave. The hole where screaming metal beasts have silenced and will never return.

We stood there and Wando once again went a few paces in front of me, raising a front leg.

"There's a dog that lives on the other side," I said. "I used to think it was just Wando. Barking down the tunnel. But she does not bark. In all the time I have been with her, she never barked once."

We did try listening for this other dog. But Bride's Cave stayed black and silent.

I asked Susan if there was a dog out there. Beyond the darkness. A dog calling for Wando to her end and she said, there was.

"When I was your age, we argued about Bride's Cave. Some said it led to the other world and is dangerous. Others have said that dogs still live out there. Dogs that we have forgotten and they have forgotten about us."

"Forgotten?"

"We believe there are ghosts on the railways. They hold you down and you cannot get away. A long time ago when people and animals lived slow and trains—fast, many died. They were killed by the ghosts and Steel Beasts, which is what the old people on the island still call the trains. Steel Beasts were big, made hissing noises and sometimes even screamed like a rooster. And yet people and especially the cows would not move. Pulling, shouting and kicking made no difference. It was as if they were glued to the tracks. The most famous victim was a wealthy bride. She was killed inside her carriage, along with the four men carrying her.

"After this the special dogs were called in. *Miewgau*, we called them. This means: railway dog. The *miewgau* lived on the railway and their job was to keep evil away. Whenever someone walked the tracks and was held down by the unseen, the dogs would come to assist. They would fight the ghosts. Fight the fear and thus, release that person or animal from the grip so the oncoming Steel Beast did not kill them.

"It was like this for a long time. But after the trains left we forgot about them."

I looked at Wando and wondered whether she was *miewgau* but Susan shook her head.

"I saw a railway dog once. In a photo. It carried a charm across its back which comes from the old days of the railway. It looks like a sword but is not really a sword. It was put there by a sacred rite so that evil could see and also the train drivers, especially from above. This sword charm was bright and shiny and was made of special steel.

"Wando was raised here--yes, but by the last nun. She has never seen a train before. Have you?"

She looked down at Wando and Wando looked back, moving her tail.

"Dogs have always haunted Bride's Cave. I think they still do."

But still, I liked to believe. Wando was incapable of hounding a big cow off the tracks because she never barked yet all the same I felt she was *miewgau*. Perhaps a distant cousin. Why would she have saved all those fish and carried them back to sea otherwise?

"The dog is strong in you," Susan said fondly, meaning Wando. "She wants to take you into Brides Cave. I think she wants to take us both."

It was then that I slowly looked at Susan, saying, "I will go if you will…"

To this she laughed, putting her hand on my head. "Perhaps one day. Perhaps in there we will understand what the wooden sword is all about…"

I nodded, smiling back. "But first we must climb that tower,"

She looked to where I was pointing.

"The bell tower? Why?"

We began walking and on the way Susan said she did not know much about the bell tower but I said I did.

"My Great Aunty built this tower. These symbols are brick talk. It says somewhere up there, in that empty space is a "room". We can't see this room but I have this funny feeling."

"Funny feeling?"

"Yes. I am afraid of the tower. I am afraid of what lives up there but I know I must climb and get to those two trees. I know there is a "room". I am Joan and this is Joan station."

Susan again looked at me funny.

"You are scared but you are Joan and this is Joan station?"

Slowly she began to laugh and so did I.

"But how are we to get this rope up there?"

I picked up the long bow leaning below the symbols which I had made.

"We use this," I said.

The bow was my second try. The first one I made being not long enough to fit the arrow which was a long steel rod I found.

We began by tying the rope to the steel rod which I think was once part of a fence. This we then fired. I let Susan do most of the shooting because she was stronger and taller.

The bell tower had five floors and we were aiming for the third floor and its window because there were no ground level windows wide enough for us to climb through.

It took Susan several shots hitting the wall and bringing down stone and leaves before it finally passed through and secured itself on the other side. I watched her pull at the rope to make sure. Then taking off her skirt to hang on a nearby bush she began to climb.

I did not take off my skirt but I did take the spyglass and an extra braided rope I made out of natal grass.

I watched Susan carefully put her right foot followed by her left into each of the holes in the wall. She did not look down at me at all but kept going.

"Mind the birds nest!" I cried.

"What?"

"In the hole. Not far from you. Do you see it?"

She took a moment before answering.

"I see it!"

I smiled.

After this I said nothing more. I waited till she reached the window and went over it with a shout.

Now came my turn. I picked up the spyglass and looked up the tower. I paused. One of the many sounds I will always remember about Joan station is the sound of air. The tall trees that grew around the station caught the high winds so always there was the sound of air. This gentle murmur was all I could hear as I pulled at the rope.

I placed my right foot into the lowest hole. I remember the first time I did this I barely managed ten holes. Now I could get all the way up to the third floor window thinking nothing of it and would have but for one reason: the holes were spaced too far from the window. This was why I needed the rope. The rope not only made the climb easier but also led straight up to the window. As I have said, the holes zigzagged in a playful way but with each step I could see Susan come to me closer and closer till at last her long hair was in my eyes and she pulled me in.

"Alright now?"

"Yes, thank you."

The first thing I noticed was how cozy it felt. The room was small and the floor was made of wood, as was the narrow staircase. Quickly we hauled up the rope and moved up the staircase, which moaned and creaked.

"Do you think anyone lives up there?"

Susan paused. "who do you think lives up there?"

There was of course, nothing there. The fourth floor was empty, as were the other floors below us. And yet throughout the whole of that summer I would go on hearing the wings flap followed by footsteps coming down, sometimes even by day. The only filled space was the top floor or belfry, where the big bell was hanging. We walked around the bell touching it, which had not been touched nor rung for such a long time yet it felt like it should be rung.

"This is marvelous," I said.

I picked up the spyglass and looked around. I liked looking through the spyglass. In the spyglass there lives another world. A world where the far off blinking lights of the sea stay still and don't blink. And the dark, scary places such as a tunnel comes close but is made safe.

Susan also liked looking through the spyglass though I am not sure if she saw other worlds as I did.

"It's so sad no one lives here," I said. "No one to make it ring."

"It's too far," Susan answered. "The trains have gone and it's too high and too far for people to walk."

I suppose we could have shot at the trees from down below but it is much easier to hit a target when you are at the same level, which the tower was. But more than anything I was curious about the tower so this in a way was a wish come true.

Throughout the summer until the time I left the island we would spend much time inside the belfry. I remember the wind in our hair and the world through the tops of trees and four tiny windows but at that moment there was no time.

Already we could see the ocean turning amber. We therefore returned to the third floor and from its west window, fired another arrow. This shot was near perfect. It went straight through the branches and held on fast after we pulled at the rope.

With the rope secured it was now time to go back down and let the rope drop so that it would dangle at the base of the tree.

It was good that we shot at the third floor because the second floor held only half a floor. It was mezzanine. When we reached the ground floor we found no windows and very dark corners, meaning the only light that came was from above the second floor window where the void was.

There was never a lock on the door of the tower and soon I found out why. It was bolted from the inside! How someone could have bolted a door from the inside I do not know. It was very mysterious. Through dim light we pulled at the bolt which was both rusty and tight. Everything was so dark and quiet until we turned the bolt. The bolt yelled and the door screamed and I felt certain the whole island must have heard us. When at last the door swung open, which also moaned very loud, we raced down the cliff to where the rope was.

"Be careful now," Susan warned.

But this I did not pay attention to for I was Joan and this was Joan station. I knew my Great Aunty had left something and it was up to me to find out.

The tree stood high above me and from it was our rope, just beyond my reach. Once more with the help of Susan I took this rope and was finally on my way. It was hot and hard going at first because there were no holes to put my foot in. But I knew things would be cooler at the top, where the winds and high branches held sway. The knots in the rope were very useful. Without it I doubt I would have climbed so quick or so easily. When at last I reached the first set of branches I stopped and sat there bathed in my own sweat. I sat breathing hard but satisfied. I looked far down below and saw Susan looking back up. I waved and she did likewise.

Soon I was onto another set of branches, the branches that looked the same as the other tree. It was here that the winds suddenly grew quite fierce and made me feel a storm was on its way. The branches swayed to and thro and I was scared. I hesitated, waiting for the winds to abate but it did not. I carried on. I turned a corner. As I did so it suddenly felt brighter, as if I had climbed into somewhere else.

7

A "ROOM" is either empty or lived in or contains something. I found something in that tree. It had the shape of a sword and seemed to be coated in wax and amber.

At first I did not touch it. I sat on the branch for sometime holding onto the rope and wondering whether I was dreaming. It certainly felt like one because the leaves moved fierce around me and yet all I could hear was a light breeze. The thing was well carved into the tree like a window. There were also other markings there that looked like it could have been made by woodpeckers. I looked at it for sometime, my heart beating fast. When finally I did move in and take the sword the wind changed tempo, as if it could finally breathe again. The blade was blunt and the whole thing was very smooth, with no difference between blade or handle or guard, which meant it was very nice to hold. Also the entire thing was very polished and shone bright like a mirror. I wondered for a moment whether this was the railway charm we have forgotten.

I tucked it over my back and into my belt then started my way down.

I scampered excitedly down the trunk eager to show Susan my discovery but instead I found Wando.

"Oh good," I said and smiled. "You will do nicely!" I put the blade next to her body for size, but my hopes were quickly dashed. It was too long. This was not meant for her.

I found Susan all the way back up the belfry where she said she could not see me.

I said I did not understand and she said, "I kept calling you. Couldn't you hear me? You said you were on that branch. But there was no one there. I kept calling you but you did not answer,"

To this day I do not know who put the sword in the tree, the spot where Susan said I disappeared from view. Was it my Great Aunty? I could not see who else it could have been. Whatever it was, I was glad something was there to be found.

I held it with both my hands which, as I have said, was very nice to hold. Susan also took hold of it, but slowly and with care. She did not say anything at first. She simply held it under the last rays of the sun. But I could tell she was very pleased with my discovery.

"Could this be a railway charm?"

Slowly she looked at me.

"I think it is," she answered. "And you found it. You found what no one knew was here…" Then she looked me in the eyes and smiling wide said, "You ought to be congratulated!" which made me feel very shy.

She put her hand on my shoulder and gave me back what I found. I smiled.

"I think I will give it a name," I said. "I will call it Wanda-Aw," which in our language means: "*discover me*".

Susan said she liked the name and I did too. For suddenly the history of trains, swords and dogs felt real.

It was a very exciting day. But the next day was not the same.

8

THE DAY was windy and dull. We were coming back from the beach when a man stood on the opposite platform. Since I was not accustomed to seeing people this alone would have frightened me to death. Yet this was not just any man. It was the Sawback, meaning the horrible man who tied dogs to the walls of empty houses.

Quickly I turned and yelled at Wando.

"Go! Run!" For I did not want her to be chained up looking dirty and perhaps even die like the bones I saw.

Up until that point I had never yelled at her, but I was very glad she understood and ran. I watched her dash off down the leafy slope and was quickly out of sight.

It was clear to me why this man was here. It was revenge. Both for taking a photo he did not like and, for speaking my mind about something that is clearly wrong. I also knew what he would say and do. And what he did say was:

"This is private property and you are trespassing!" He then said he would take me to the police, but at the last moment changed his mind. He only said he would call the police should he see me here again. But what he did take from me was the key, meaning I would never come into see Wando again.

Always from the beginning I expected someone would order me to get out but never did I expect it to be him, the mean man who was cruel to dogs. The very same man who would end my happy time at the secret station.

I suppose he must have seen me head up to the station many times and it was only a matter of time before he followed and found out my secret.

I packed my bags and walked out the gate under glaring eyes, but not far. Once he had gone I came back. I stood outside the lock gate thinking about Wando and began to cry.

I did not want to cry. But I had to.

Always before I feared Wando might go into Bride's Cave but now there was a new fear, one that was greater than the fear of forgetting. I was not to stay on Joan Island forever. What if one day after I have left that man returned and chained Wando like his other dogs?

9

I SAT on my suitcase. I sat there watching Wando who had returned and looked at me from the other side of the locked gate. It felt to me like my first day back on the island.

"Don't worry," I said. "I won't leave you. We will think of a way…"

I stayed outside the gate. I did not know what else I could do. I stayed and listened to the winds hum. I listened and listened until I heard a pair of light footsteps coming up the hill where nobody walked. I looked. It was Susan. Coming up the path.

I was no longer crying now but when she saw me and said, "*Oy yoy yoy* what

a sad face!" I could not help myself.
I burst into tears.

"What is the matter? *What* happened?"
Holding back my sobs I explained how
I had lost the key. And that I had
ruined our chance of a happy summer.

"I know now why she needs to go," I
said. "She is looking for her voice.
She must have lost it in Bride's
Cave. A dog cannot fight evil with no
bark. But it's too late now. I cannot
help her. The key is gone. I have
missed my chance..."

Susan did not do nor say anything at
first. She knelt down next to me and
smiled. I felt her hand at my
shoulder. She spoke.

"Wando lost her voice, you say. But don't you know if you answer a voice in the dark you will be forever under its dark spell and be sucked in? If Bride's Cave does already have Wando's voice as you say, then Wando can never answer so what is there to be sad about?

"I could not read Wando's future because it is dark, like a cave. I could see nothing. But that is not a bad thing. We can change that. We can do something.

"You are the saddest looking girl in the world right now. But that…" she paused to look at her watch, "can change, also. What if I told you the next moment you will be the happiest girl in the world?"

I looked up, wondering what she meant.

"Do you know why?"

I shook my head. She then asked to see all of my pictures which I kept inside my suitcase. All the ones I have taken since coming to the island. I did not understand but I opened my case all the same. There were about thirty. She looked through them all. Through her big glasses she looked hard. Her brows pulled tight saying, "*Nein…nein…nein,*" one after the other and before long even I joined in, saying *nein…nein…nein* and laughing as if it were a very funny song. When at last she found the one she wanted she smiled excitedly and said, "Yes! This is the one!"

I looked. But still I did not understand. It was the picture of the gate key.

"Wando was only a pup when she began walking pilgrims down this lonely path. Now with this picture you have taken it is our turn to help Wando find her path the way she helped others. We will take this photo to the key maker. He will make us a new key. And with this new key, you and I will go with Wando into Bride's Cave. Would you like that?"

My eyes lit up. Finally I got it. I jumped up and clasp both my hands together in delight, shouting, "Yes please!"

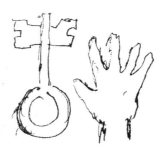

BOOK II
The Place of Hallo

10

IT WAS LATE in the day when we began our journey. We broke through into Bride's Cave by taking a heavy branch and ramming it, which was all it took. Suddenly at our feet was a pile of dried, flaky wood light as paper, which is what happens to timber when termite have been through.

I had packed well for the journey. Enough food for many days and of course my camera, plus an extra two pack of films making a total of twenty two films including the six that was already in the camera. But that was not what made my pack heavy. It was the sword and drinking water of which I kept in four canteens, of which two of them was carried by Wando. Susan too brought food and water and a fair share of her own burden.

"This is Henry," she said. "My neighbour's rooster." She put down the big bird saying he too, like Wando will protect us on our journey.

I liked Henry. He had a big, red crown and eyes that seemed to look at you all the time. It was good to have Henry for protection, in the same way it was good to have Wando and the sword and of course Susan who, like myself knew what it means to have protection.

Over her pack she carried one arrow that she made and the one bow I made, which she would later improve by adding a handle and notch as a guiding platform for the arrow.

But this was not the kind of protection I meant.

"Tika" is a small, red magic circle. A circle which Susan often wore across her forehead which she now made all of us, including Henry even though he was male and had the smallest head, wore the same. I liked having Tika a lot because it made me look like Susan which also made us look like sisters.

"The sword will weigh you down, you know?" she said. But at the same time she knew as well as I that this was one burden I had to bear. For the sword was our key. Without it there would be no adventure.

"Remember. There are no windows inside. Nothing to see but darkness and empty space where it is not meant for walking. Are you ready?"

I said nothing. Taking the sword charm in one hand and Susan's hand in the other, I simply gave a slow nod.

We set off. I do not know if Henry knew what was going on but for Wando it was a moment she had been waiting for, for a very long time. She was already far out ahead of us and setting a good pace. I watched her being quickly swallowed up by darkness that we would soon become.

Everything went dark. Even the bricks were, the ones that Susan said was left by the steam locomotives of long ago when smoke and screams filled the tunnel. Yet black was not to be the only colour that filled our being. There was brown, copper, green and even white leaking down like fissures. But no grass at all, not even a bat.

To save batteries we used just the one torch. The spare we would use later. But I did not have to rely on torchlight to know we were leaving Joan Island far behind. I could feel it in the air. As we walked deeper it became cool and windless. Soon there was nothing around us but sound. The sound from our footsteps and some times water that leaked from above.

I remember how afraid I was the first time I stood in front of the tunnel. My mind full of strange thoughts but now it was different. A rooster, a dog and a magic weapon, made it different. I was in good company and was therefore very excited. It was probably because of this I began to talk loud. *We* began to talk loud.

"*Hello!*"

"*Are you having a nice time?*"

"*Yes I am thank you!*"

Tunnels are good places to make sound but we were very surprised at how our voices quaked. It was like a big wave spilling out followed by splashes in the way of water. It was so loud that I was certain this would frighten Wando but she did not even turn her head to look back at us.

Not long after this I stepped on something that made a bigger noise than we.

"*CRACK!*"

It shot down the tunnel like a windy spear.

We shone the torch. I looked down and picked up something. It was a large plastic bottle. How it got in there I do not know but it sounded very much like the bone crack I often heard when standing outside Bride's Cave, which it probably was.

"By day when it is hot the bottle expands. But by night when it is cool it contracts. It is possible what you heard was this plastic bottle."

If that is what it was, one mystery was solved, but not the barking dog.

Since the walk was long and dark, we talked about many other things, especially about the railway and its dogs.

"The cow would not get off the railway and so the dog barked. It hounded the big beast who in turn swung its big horns. In the end the cow left the tracks but later the dog died."

"Died?"

"Yes. People used to farm beside the tracks and put down poison. This dog while hounding the bull walked over poison. When later it went to lick its paws it ate this poison and so died."

"But that is so sad," I said, almost frowning. And yet, I was not sad about it for long. Behind us I could hear Henry making his *clucks* while in front was Wando trotting and being very bold about it as if there was nothing to fear. They too were telling us stories here and now. And what stories they were.

At one point Henry began to crow. The sound filled the tunnel like a train whistle but not so sharp. It was long and hollow, with some bass notes at the end. We did not understand at first and just laughed, but then slowly came other bird sounds and we knew the other side was close, and it was.

A pinhole appeared which soon got bigger and bigger.

When at last we stepped out into hot light my eyes went wide.

Always Bride's Cave echoed with the cry of distant gulls. Now I could see them. They were flying above and under us. Under, because there was a bridge and we were standing on it. I blinked and could hardly believe my eyes. At the other side of Bride's Cave was a long and forgotten sea bridge!

"There will be many more," Susan said. "They link other islands. Joining it like a peninsula."

The thought of one bridge crossing the sea was enough but many? I stared. My heart beating fast. Always when I thought about Bride's Cave I thought about what I could hear and not what I could see. The bridge was old and had something like a face where creepers and bushes had grown upon it but it seemed to be built well and meant to last and this it had.

I walked over to where Wando was standing and looking back at us, as if again waiting for us to come.

"I wish to see what you see," I said. "I wish to go where you go..."

"And now you will," was what Susan finally said.

We found no dog barking but even if there was we would have crossed the bridge anyway because it was there that we found paw prints. They were dried mud prints left on the sleepers and partly hidden by grass. I did not know what animal it was. Perhaps it was a dog. A dog that stood there and barked which I could hear when I was on the other side. Now all we had to do was find the creature.

Wando again, was far out in front of us. She was so eager to explore that she did not even stop after all four of her legs fell through the gaps in the sleeper. It was a cattle grid. But she did not care. After hitting her chin she quickly bounced back up and carried on as if nothing had happened.

This made me smile because it looked like she was dancing on fire and this it probably was. The sea under us was ablaze. Probably more so in my mind because most of the time I could not see it. The bridge had low walls on both sides but to me it was not low. All I could see was the sky which made me feel as if I were flying with the gulls. I therefore walked the whole length of the bridge still thinking the sea was ablaze when really the fire had gone.

When we came to the end and the sea had faded we found ourselves in a small valley. I looked back at the darkened tracks to see how far we had

travelled and raised my sword. There was no way the Lock Man could come for me now and take me to the police. That much was certain.

We came to a place of trees that grew up the stone valley. We chose this because there was a small crack of running water. This we used for washing and drinking while the trees allowed us to string up our hammocks in a V which meant we could sleep beside one another, almost head to head. Once this was done and Susan began cooking, Wando and I went about collecting strong smelling flowers and sedges to make a large magic circle around the fire. This I was sure would protect us as we slept, for there were endless numbers of glowing eyes that stared back at us.

I forgot to pack my tooth brush so I asked Susan if I could borrow hers.

"If you don't mind," she said.

The only member of our team that was not in the magic circle that night was Henry. I had not heard from him for sometime. The last thing I remember was looking back at Bride's Cave and hearing *Cockadoodado!*

"He will come in his own time," Susan said. "Birds do things in their time. The way they see time is different."

11

IT WAS FUNNY she said that because in the morning it was Henry who woke me. All night the sea sounded below us like a whisper but now it was Henry's turn. His crow was again loud, slow and very bassy. After the third crow I rose.

"Good morning, Henry!" I said. "where did you go last night?"

Peck, peck, peck was the only answer I got for he was too busy pecking for insects.

I climbed down from my hammock and rattled the spoon and plate that was hanging off it. I put on my shoes. I looked down the tracks both ways. There were no trains and no sign of the others. I took my camera and quickly went about looking for them.

The sun was not yet high but the grasshoppers were already buzzing. I walked along the bushy ridge calling for Susan and Wando. After some moments I heard a rustle then a head appeared. It was a dog carrying a wooden toy sword.

"There you are!" I said. I picked at one of the strange flowers and gave it to her. She sniffed. I then took the trail she had made and soon found a humpbacked bridge and what looked like a lighthouse, the strangest I have ever seen.

I could see someone standing at the top waving. It looked like Susan and she was pointing to what looked like a door.

I waved back and walked to the door. The door was tall and it was open. I entered and the first thing I saw was a stairway. It spiraled up into the lighthouse and was made of steel.

It was quiet inside but as we began climbing the round staircase passed the round wall I heard the sea again. It was coming from a big round hole.

This hole should have told me that this was no lighthouse. But again I was too busy watching Wando. Stairs after all, was her life: going up and down the stairs to the beach and the water front. I watched her go up the steps two to three at a time, and was quite fast once she got into the stride of things.

I still had no idea what I was climbing until I got to the top. There was a large bell not unlike the one back at the station. But this one had a telephone and Susan was standing next to it. The phone itself was old fashion and it was placed upon a stone pedestal specially made for it. At first she asked if I wanted to call home and I wondered which home? For now I felt I had many.

Then she asked, "Did you notice the windmill on your way up?" and I replied I did. Facing the large hole which I had passed was a large propeller, like a windmill blade but inside the tower. "I think this is a storm house and that propeller is what makes the tower ring. When a storm comes and the winds pick up this tower rang and so warned the trains to stop running."

"A warning?"

"A warning," answered Susan.

I was surprised at first to hear and see such a thing. But then I looked around myself. An island. Something that is famous for storms. We were to come across many other storm houses along the way and we climbed many of them wondering how fast the winds would have to be before the windmill spun hard enough to make the heavy bell ring and whether being neglected for so long it could still ring. But none of them had a telephone like the first one did. I picked up this phone to see if by chance it might work. I heard a click. But it was not the click of a telephone. It was a camera. Susan had taken a photo.

12

THE MORNING was hot and humid. Already the animals were panting. Wando through her tongue and Henry, by moving his throat. We headed towards the sun, walking from one island to the next, just as Susan said we would.

These islands were all rock with no beaches of any kind for they shot out of the sea like blades. It were these rock blades that the old railway stood upon which meant we were always hundreds of feet in the air. But the oddest part was the trees. They grew everywhere. On cliffs and impossible angles, yet they never took hold upon the railway itself. Grass grew there, but never trees. The only time trees came on the tracks was when it grew over it and even then it was in the shape of a rough tunnel as if locomotives were still coming through which it was not.

The railway charm came in useful after all. With it I slashed my way down the track, hacking at brambles and bushes which were the things that got in our way the most. Susan too carried a blade of her own. It was very sharp but short, and the blade was curved.

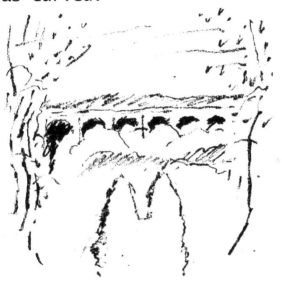

Mostly I was trying to beat out grasshoppers that were very numerous. Grasshoppers like the sun. They sing and buzz when the birds do not. I

have no idea how many insects a
chicken can eat in one day but we
caught many and not once did Henry
refuse our catch even though he was a
far better hunter than we were.

Wando did not chase grasshoppers but
she did chase a large bird that ran
fast. It was very funny because the
bird was shaped like a calabash, but
on legs! I had never seen her do this
before on Joan Island probably
because there were no fast running
land birds there.

Another bird, who was black with
long legs flew up and down like a
yoyo. We saw it far down the tracks
and was probably the strangest thing
I have ever seen a bird do.

We walked from island to island, from one sun to the next all the time thinking and feeling we would see no one. But then we began to see wild cows. Cows were living on the railway! A herd of them ran from us when they saw our approach. They went thundering down the tracks and broke the silence.

Now it was clear to us why the railway was so clean. The cows had kept it clean by munching their way down the line. It was a delight seeing the cows because they were very funny. They munched everything, even cactus!

But it was seeing old houses that surprised and frightened me the most. Crumbling old houses they were. The first one was right beside the tracks and we wondered whether it was a ruined station. The later ones stood further away down the line, on a cliff or a hill. We looked into some of these hill ones but did not enter, fearing the roofs might collapse and fall.

"People lived here?"

"Long ago they did. They lived and farmed here. Look. They even farmed the slopes. Anywhere there was earth. But when the railway came and left they too left this behind."

I could not see how people could have lived somewhere so lonely and with so little land, and storms beating against the rocks. But as Susan had said, clearly there were people. For without them there would have been no cows to plough their terraces which have now gone wild the same way the cows have and was probably the reason why the grass around the railway have not turned into a jungle for the cows must have ate them and kept them short.

It was hard to breathe at times. The sun baked and heat blurred the tracks. Only when we came under thick trees did we feel cool, as if we had suddenly walked into Autumn.

By afternoon we had crossed five bridges and a trestle. The trestle spanned a jagged ravine and was all made of old wood. There were no side barriers which meant we had to walk with care or else, fall into the sea. But there were long planks running over the gaps in the sleepers which made the crossing easier if not safer.

It was while we were on this trestle that I heard Susan shout,

"*Train!*"

My heart jumped. Quickly I looked back over my shoulders.

There was of course, no train and never will be. Yet still, it was very funny.

I carried the spyglass around my neck on a string and with this I looked across the sea. The sea was all around us and yet the railway was often cut into the valley meaning the sea was out of sight. I asked Susan what stones made the strange mountains and she said, "Limestone."

"Do limestone have protein?"

"Protein?"

"How do plants grow up there? With no soil."

"There is soil," she said. Though at the time she did not know how it got there. Only much later did we find out how. Grass and sedges cling to limestone and die. When they die they rot and leave behind protein and seeds and this process is repeated many, many times over till this rot becomes soil high on the stone ledge.

There were seeds that grew into flowers and trees. And sedges tall enough to catch sunlight and look pretty. But our favourite was the sticky weed or bur sedge. We threw many different sedges at one another to see if they would stick but more so at Wando because she never complained. Probably because they never really stuck to her thin summer coat.

There were monkeys with pointy heads and birds with pointy heads, too.

There were also rocks shaped like animals. One we could see was clearly in the shape of a giant toad.

I spotted a few ships but they were too far and we could not wave to them. We did wave to a flock of birds who looked to be heading north, the same way we were.

About this time a hum rose in the air that made me feel uneasy. The noise filled the stone walls above us as if they would bring down rocks. I knew this was the humming of bees but did not know why until I picked up my spyglass. They were fighting! In balls of maybe ten or twenty bees they fought, and so fixed they were in their rolling they cared not about the birds that were pecking at them for food. But no matter how many they pecked the bees remained a cloud.

Susan and I looked at one another.

There seemed to be no way of getting pass. No way, that is until Susan spotted a way of getting up the tunnel arch. It stood on the other side of the swirling bees, like a ridge way.

"Wait here," she told me. "I won't be long."

I did as she said and went and sat down behind shade.

I watched her go behind a big rock but did not remember any else because I fell asleep.

I woke with a crab crawling under me. I rubbed my eyes and slowly picked it up. The crab was red. It did not move fast and nor did it pinch me. Far below us lived mangroves and I suspect it must have crawled up one of the trees. I put it to one side, hoping Henry would not attack. He did not!

Dack-yee are words that mean sweet or pleasant. This mangrove was *dack-yee* because of the strange green, turnip fruits growing there. It would be a good place to explore, perhaps later on our way back.

Not far a voice was calling my name. It came down the valley through the buzzing of grasshoppers in a very empty way as if we were the only people left in the whole world. I turned from the mangroves and looked up. A figure was waving to me. High above the tunnel arch.

"*HAALLO, JOOAN!*" it said.

Quickly I waved back.

"*HAALLO, SUUSAN!*"

Since we were sweating so much we stopped often to drink, not just for ourselves but for the animals. The way a bird drinks is funny. They must bring their heads down and then tilt far back in order to swallow. We watched Henry do this. And Wando, who lapped noisily at the tray until it was empty.

I wondered about Henry often. I wondered whether this was the first time he had ever seen a railway. I did not have to wonder much about Wando because somewhere out there was another dog which we had yet to find.

We drank often and because of this our canteens were soon close to being empty. And this being only our second day!

There were many red berries, but the only ones fit to eat, Susan said were shaped like a bird's foot. Tree sap was also good because I saw Wando licking globes of it. They looked

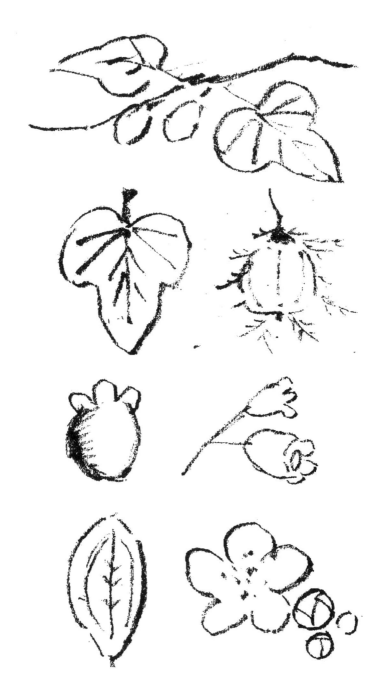

like rock sugar and tasted almost the same. Yet the strangest water it seemed, came from a root. It was growing under the sand and looked almost like a long potato.

"I have heard of this root," Susan told me. "But I did not think it was true!"

The first one we dug up we grated. And from this we squeezed the juice into a bowl.

The juice was milky brown but quite sweet, yet between the four of us it was not enough. Water was all around us but none of it was fit to drink. We had to find drinking water and soon.

There were things along the railway that looked like huge tap heads but none of them held any water. I liked the way how Wando would sit by these things and wait for us. Her body so composed and calm like a triangle.

As I have said, there was no way of getting down to the sea but we did find one.

The way down was steep with gnarled bushes but we had to go down because of Wando. Many calabash quails were running down the tracks and she must have been chasing one. It was late in the afternoon now. Lizards were clambering about. They hunted among the jagged rocks and I even saw one catch a butterfly. I had never seen this and excited, I pointed this out to Susan.

At last we came down to a ledge. It hung just above the green water, next to a water cave. Henry who was not far behind us again began to crow. The sound echoed around the cave in a very deep and frightening manner as if the cave had never heard such a cry before.

Then Susan said she could see something on the other side.

"It looks like a chest," she said. "Underwater. I am going to have a look,"

I was excited about the chest under water but not the water. Through the spyglass I could see a large dark patch in the water that was not too far from where Susan wanted to go. I passed the spyglass to Susan but she did not see the same thing.

"It is only shadow," she said.

She put her clothes to one side and jumped in. The sound she made was deep like a hollow well but bigger. After this the silence returned and she swam with grace, quietly to the other side. I too put my dress next to hers and was about to follow her splash when at the last moment I again picked up the spyglass.

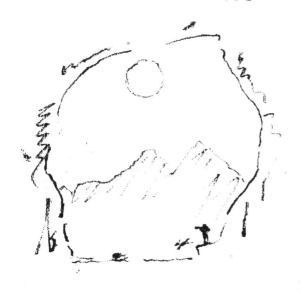

The black shape was still there but this time it was moving. This time it looked like something big that was alive.

I let go of the spyglass. I wanted to yell out loud and warn Susan but she was already under water.

The shape was very close now. Before I could think of what else to do another splash sounded. I looked and there in the water was Wando, paddling her feet. Back on Joan Island we never swam very far because of sharks. She must have jumped in because Susan did.

The shape drifted. I thought that by some chance Wando had diverted the shape's attention. It did not. I felt certain it was now coming for Susan. When at last she broke the surface for air I screamed at the top of my voice.

"Behind you!"

My voice tore through the lagoon like thunder. She looked.

I thought that she might glance back to see what I was pointing at. She did not. Instead she quickly swam my way and in no time climbed back onto the ledge.

By now the dark patch was already passing under Wando. I watched terrified. My breath held. Fortunately that was all it did do. We stood and fearfully watched it slowly pass us by. It was long and dark, like a giant submarine.

I was sure Wando knew nothing of what had happened because afterwards she did not raise one leg and look across the sea.

"Did you find anything?" I asked.

She shook her head. "Only this,"

She held up a broken piece of curved metal.

That night we camped by a stream. It flowed out of the rocks and went under the tracks, through a stone bridge.

I fell to my knees on a curve in the sand bank.

In seeing this Susan said, "You must be very tired,"

I looked up. I shook my head. I was very tired but the swallows darting above us lifted my spirits and soon I was on my feet again. There was wood to collect, food to cook and a magic circle to make. The circle was the easiest to do because the sand was soft. Since we had not washed properly the night before and our canteens were near empty this camp was the perfect place to make our preparations for the next day.

Before going to sleep as a treat Susan told me another story.

At first she began by saying, "You know, Joan Island was named after a girl..."

But I turned and looked at her.

"Once upon a time. You must start with once upon a time. A good story always begins with once a upon time..."

I could not see Susan. She was just a slow voice in the dark now. But I could tell she was smiling because almost everything I said and did made her smile, especially at my making of a magic circle that would protect us every night.

"Once upon a time there was a young girl with golden hair. She rowed out to sea in a storm, with a dog by her side. Why did she row out in a storm? She was rowing out to ask the gods of the sea to stop people making animal sacrifices to the sea. Cows, birds and fish were offered to the sea because the sea and its storms is a power no one can control. Nothing was ever heard of the girl or the dog again. The name of the girl was Joan. This is how Joan Island was named."

"But why did the dog have to go to sea?" I asked slowly for I was now feeling very sleepy.

"She did not. It followed her. When she rowed away the dog followed. It swam to her boat and she had no choice but to pull it aboard."

"It was her dog, then?"
"I think so."

I fell asleep thinking about this swimming dog but what I really thought of was Wando swimming above a dark shadow.

Somewhere in the night I was woken by strange noises but the soft voice of the sighing sea far down below made me forget and I slept soundly. But in the morning I found tracks. They were in the sand and had hooves in them. This meant it was probably made by wild hogs. There were also tracks of a dog mixed in with the hogs which meant Wando had probably chased them off. Henry had probably seen them too for he had mounted himself upon a bush. They do this because a rooster is still a bird and high places make them feel safe.

So far we had seen bird tracks, cow tracks, goats, deer and even strange shadows in the water but never again did we see the dog prints we saw on the other side of Bride's Cave. We did not see not because they were not there. Perhaps it was because there were too many fun things to look at.

13

WE RAN into the cows again the next day. It was very early in the morning when the sun had barely risen but this time they did not thunder away. They seemed determined to stay at this one spot which appeared to have an opening in the rock face.

Since they would not get out of our way we took this opening thinking it might detour around the cows. It was very steep but through a long twist we soon made it to the top where we found a stranded calf. It was standing outside a cave and had probably been there all night.

Perhaps this was why the cows would not leave.

The calf we would rescue but first we wanted to see the cave. The opening was shaped like a tadpole, while inside it sounded like running water. We left our packs behind and the only thing I carried was the sword. Susan had the torch. It was dark and twisty at first but as we got further in it began to waver and glow like water.

I turned around and looked up. A shaft of early morning sunlight was coming in above us and was hitting a small spot at the back of the cave filled with running water.

The light came in at an angle which meant I could reach up and touch it but when I did, the back of the cave turned dull.

Since my palm was brightly lit I knew there was something else that could be even brighter.

I raised the sword above my head and kept it there. Instantly the light was turned. It was now lighting up a dark ledge above us which we did not know was there.

Slowly I moved the blade from left to right shinning up many shapes and patterns carved into the rock.

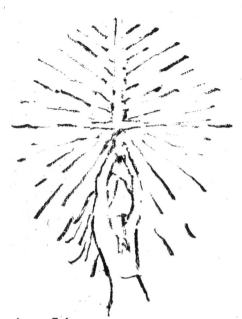

The lines went over and under one another like the sea which at first looked like erosion but the more we looked the more it looked like it was made by people.

I could see fish, boats and perhaps even people with spears.

It was strange to see the first rays of dawn inside a cave and I wondered how long the shapes must have remained unseen until we came.

We carried down the forlorn looking calf thinking the calf's mother would be happy to see it. But instead the mother pushed it away and would not let the calf come close.

"Perhaps it's not her calf," I said.

"Perhaps it's too old for milk," was what Susan said. "It wants to keep suckling mummy but mummy thinks it is time to stop being a baby."

The rest of the morning we spent gathering sumac. Sumac is a flower that makes salt early in the morning.

"Salt is necessary," Susan said, "Sweat takes away salt in the body. If salt is not replenished you will feel sick and tired."

I asked Susan how she knew so much about such things and she said, "In the old days wild plants was all the island had. Today it is very strange for people to pick and use wild flowers but in my grandmother's time everyone did the same."

I was therefore under no doubts to why I was feeling very replenished when we came across something else from the railway.

Of all the half buried things we found: posts, hooks, levers, sundials and flagstones, some even carved with names *this* was probably the closet thing to what a railway means.

It was lying slanted to one side under a big over hanging rock looking almost like a boat on a beach. The hand car is like a go cart but on rails. It was built to carry out maintenance along the tracks meaning you could easily lift it on and off the tracks. The one we found had rusted wheels and the wood on it was dried and cracked just like an old boat. It had not been used for so long that potter wasps had left many of their tiny pots stuck to the wood. We doubted it would run but I had never seen a hand car before and nor have I ever ridden one.

"I think this was meant for us," Susan said.

"It's been waiting for us for a long time," I said.

"Come. Let's see if it works."

It was very hot now and we wasted no time. We grabbed the handles and, lifting it like a wheel barrow, pushed it onto the tracks to see if it would work. Sadly it did not, but it was fun to try nevertheless. The lever which pumped and moved the wheels was seized. And when we did manage to move it a little, it made a screeching sound so bad I had to cover my ears.

We abandoned the car in the end but came back to it in the afternoon. We came back because we found oil. We found it inside a storm house further down the tracks. Since the first storm house contained old tools and things we were certain there had to be the same inside this one and so decided to go in and have a look. At first this was not so easy to do because a fig tree was blocking the doorway. The tree had grown into the doorway and worked its way up the house meaning I had to climb the tree next to it and swing across. This Susan did not like because it looked dangerous but I liked because she was acting more and more like a big sister. And even more so when I found my way hampered by a small snake coiled around a branch.

"A what?!" she cried, looking up at me. Her eyes big and wide with concern.

The snake was not big but I went around it anyway and reached for a higher branch. What I found was, by moving my weight down this higher branch I was soon lowered and was able to grab the branches shooting out of the big round hole and clambered in but at the expense of tearing my skirt, so the snake getting in my way was probably a good thing after all.

My biggest shock turned out to be birds and not the snake. I surprised two birds as I came in. They went darting over my head from left to right while trying to get out. When finally they did get out and silence returned, I let go of my head and stood up.

"I am fine!" I cried because I could hear Susan shouting at me from down below.

There were many drums and cans in front of me now and carefully I looked through them all. The light was dim but I managed to pick out the shape of many long spouts which could only have been oil cans. I picked out two that were heavy and full. Again I was not so happy about taking something that was not mine, yet I was happy about the staircase. There was an outside staircase behind the storm house all along. If only we had known it was there it would have saved me much trouble!

I did not know if the oil would work being sat there for so long and in the heat but then Susan laughed and said,

"It's lasted millions of years right under our feet. What difference is a few more years?"

We went back to the cart and squirted the liquid into the gears and anywhere that needed oiling. It was late afternoon now.

At first we did not put down our heavy packs. We did not think it would work because the machine was so brown with rust, but slowly as we worked, the lever began to move. Bit by bit it squeaked and moved and bit by bit we felt we could add things to it. First, our heavy packs and then, a dog, and finally when we caught him, a rooster.

The cart was meant to carry two grown men and we were just two girls so there was plenty of room.

As we rumbled down the tracks picking up good speed I looked happy at Susan and she looked happy at me.

Suddenly it felt like we had wings. I would look. And the mountains and seas that one moment stood far and away in the next, would be in front and then soon behind us. In no time we were crossing from place to place, from one dark valley into another brighter valley. We even came to a place where butterflies flew fast over our heads like swifts. Then another, was a place of *fungot*, which is a root you can cook and eat. We gathered this and more, almost anything we wanted now because we no longer had the burden of carrying it ourselves. But the nicest and most *dack-yee* thing of them all, besides feeling lovely and cool was going fast, especially through dark woods.

In a way it was like riding the midnight train because a midnight train does not stop. Branches and bumps made no difference. It carried on. Sometimes in silence and some-times not. Even without our rowing it carried on probably due to the railway going downhill but I was sure that was not the only reason.

"This is a magic sword!" I said, pointing to it. "And this is a magic dog!" Pointing to the dog sat beside me. "And now we have a magic boat!"

The dog, I could see enjoyed going fast for she was leaning into the wind. The rooster, probably not so much because he could no longer peck for grubs.

Most of the time the ride was good but often the track was wonky which made it bumpy. And though the views were nice, sound such as when passing through rocks that echoed or a noisy water fall could also tell us where we were. Tall rocks and high peaks are good places for water falls and in the end this was what made us stop and make camp for the night.

We could have gone on further but it is better to mope about in daylight when all the hidden dangers of a new place could be seen.

We were tired, but in a different way. Mainly because we did not have red marks across our shoulders because of the packs.

"How much further do you think we can go?" I asked.

Susan was watching the birds fly by as though she were counting them one by one.

"We could go on forever," she said. "If you don't mind eating roots and berries…"

The roots Susan spoke of were of three different kinds. One had in it many fibres and was therefore good for soup, while the other two came out sweet and soft when roasted under the heat of a fire.

Cooking the latter two roots was my favourite. A fire is built and the roots are left under it. Although this was easy to do, it took time for they are cooked very slowly in the embers.

We did not have to make a magic circle that night. Someone else had already made one. It was made from stones of all shapes and sizes and was made around a tree. It was also probably very old because the stones had sunk into the ground and grass had grown around them.

As the last of the passing birds faded into the night I wondered about them.

"There are no trains," I said. "But there are. The birds are the new trains. Bird trains are quiet and sweet. They use the tracks just like trains but make no smoke or noise."

Susan looked and also seemed to agree.

"They fly a long way," she said. "The railway and its bridges give them a place to land and rest."

I thought I might end up dreaming about the birds but instead I kept dreaming the hand car had gone.

In the morning I told Susan of my funny dream and she laughed.

"Did you dream?"

"I will tell you later," she replied.

It was a different place now. Plants and animals were also different. There is the sticky weed named butterfly needles which is the weed of nightmares because it sticks into socks and animals and takes great patience to remove but now they were gone. I also found a crab- looking spider hitch hiking on my back pack. It was black and white and had many horns.

Black headed gulls were barking above us, which was something I never saw on Joan Island.

We watched them fly over us as if following the tracks and wondered why. The answer came late in the day.

14

THE STATION was built on top of a bridge, in the middle of the ocean. I spotted it through the spyglass long before we came to it. But that was not the most exciting part. It was the island below it.

Up until this point we had never seen an entire island made of sand before. And so bare.

We slowly rolled up to the station and stepped off while the gulls flew on. The station had a small lighthouse, which I thought was sweet, with trees along the platform and was called Diana, which means *country of giants*. It said so above the metal gate and on the platform sign post.

The place was very empty and bright so I knew we were going to have a happy time but there was one other thing that was very strange.

On each side of the platform were cannons. Both sat on wheels and both faced the sea.

"I have never seen this on a train station before," I said, but not to Susan.

"We have them back on the island. Didn't you see them? In the old days they were fired often because of pirates. This was how we kept them away."

I looked and tried to imagine the cannons and pirates but I did not think about them for long.

Sunlight was bouncing off the ocean and it was very pretty. It showered the walls of the station with glittering light and wavering shadows which made me feel as if we were standing next to a pond of light.

A zigzag of old stairs took us down to the water and from there we waded onto the beach.

We all got wet except for Henry for he did not have to wade as we did. He reached the other side by walking on water and flapping his red wings making loud noises as he went.

At first I did not understand why the station and bridge was not built upon the island itself. It stood about a hundred paces from the beach in shallow water. Only much later did we understand the island had moved.

We explored the island briefly but was soon quite certain there was no one there but us.

"*Hello!*" I shouted. "*My name is Joan and this is Susan, Wando and Henry! Is there anyone home?*" I looked past the dunes and the waves, but no reply ever came.

It was late now. The sun was hovering low on the horizon so we decided to spend a night on this strange island of white sand, not knowing that we would stay longer and that this was to be our voyage end.

Before night fell we gathered clams and netted some prawns. The prawns were fun and I could feel them shooting away from under my feet. We cooked on the platform and made camp there. We felt it was safer because there was a gate we could close and lock.

One of the first things I noticed about the island was the fragrance. It came from the grassland which stretched far but not so wide. Many flowers grew there and one of them looked like yarrow, and I think it was.

Everything was so different. Even the air was different. No longer was it hot and sticky but fresh and cool, especially being this high up. It was so nice that Wando and I stayed standing in the breeze for a long time.

Dogs like to smell. Good or bad smell makes no difference. They like both.

I watched the nose quiver. The nostrils flared as it picked up something in the air. Something was out there. Something was fun.

"What is it, Wando? What is out there?"

I picked up my spyglass and looked down at the mysterious island. It was of course too dim to see anything clearly but something was there and Wando knew this. It was moving across the sands. It looked like two large white balloons. This scared me and I went to sleep wondering what it was.

15

THE NEXT MORNING we went back to the beach to look for what it was I saw the night before. There was a bright, dreamy fog around the island and this made the animal tracks we found even more special. Most of them were along the beach but they also took place among the dunes where the marram grass grew.

"Have you ever hugged a horse?"

Susan looked at me, shaking her head.

"You must try. It's nice."

I said this because there were horses. Mustangs. Most of the tracks on the island were made by hooves. Horses have strong odour which dogs like. I was sure this must have been what I saw through the spyglass the night before.

We decided to look for them and by noon we did. They were mostly copper brown in colour. Some quite shabby looking. But as we got close they ran from us. All the living things we have seen so far from monkeys to birds and lizards, none of them cared or feared us and yet here was a common animal and they did not like us. At first I thought it was fear of people but then Susan and Wando walked up and they stayed. They did not run. But whenever I tried they ran.

It seemed that they feared only me. They all did.

I was not so puzzled or upset by this. I knew something about horses. Horses do not like things they have not seen before. I suspect it was not so much these horses living on this island shaped like a long bow had never seen a girl. It was they had never seen a girl with a sword before. I was wearing the sword on a sling across my back as I always did. This must have put fear in their hearts. And so they ran. All but save one. A very beautiful, white mare.

This mare must have been very special because she very quickly made friends with Wando. They ran along the shore splashing up water. And though she could not run as fast or as long as the mustang I have never seen a dog or horse so happy.

It was as I watched that a funny thought ran through my mind. Wando always raised her front leg like a horse. Perhaps she wished to be a horse. And that all horses were once dogs.

I told Susan this, thinking it was funny but she said, "You know what I think is really funny? We still call roads: *marlow*, meaning *horse way* but horses do not use horse ways and Joan Island has never had one."

The other thing we noticed about the island were trees. There were none. But this being an island, and islands have beaches we were certain there would be driftwoods to be had and there was.

We had thought we found ourselves a deserted island. But the rubbish found on the beach quickly changed that. Much of it was plastic. We found chairs, nets, dolls, slippers, bits of burst balloons and many cigarette lighters. The beach was long and some of this plastic even got caught around the hooves of the horses.

We therefore spent the morning picking through the plastics for bits of driftwood. The short ones we used for cooking while the long ones to make a fish trap along the shore.

We also needed clean drinking water. This station called Diana had a container but the rain water there was old. Fit to wash with but not drinking. There was a fairly large pond not too far from the station which would have been ideal. But this belonged to the horses and they were stood in it chest deep eating the waterweeds. And besides, this water was full of leeches. The only water fit to drink was at the west end of the island. There, not far from a house buried deep in sand we found a well.

"The well made by ghosts," I said. The reason why I said this is because on one of the stones around it were the words "Built by nobody!"

"It might have been built by itself," said Susan. But I felt "Ghost" sounded better. Much better than "built by Cow or sheep or crab,"

We tried to look at this house, which seemed to be the only building on the island but all there was to see was a bell feature. And even that did not work because a big sea bird had built a nest of sticks inside.

Grasshoppers were playing violins and buzzing all around us. On the way back I could not help myself and fell asleep.

When I woke I did not know where I was. I stood up. The sun was not so high now and nor was it so hot. Nearby I saw a dung beetle. These beetles were plenty because of the horses. They were always busy rolling their balls as if that was all that mattered. It was going up the tallest dune so I decided to do the same.

I bent down over on all fours and began walking backwards. It felt strange to see the world upside down but it did make me see the many different sized tracks in the sand. The beetle unfortunately did not get very far walking the way it did. About quarter of the way up it flipped over and along with its ball rolled all the way back down. I stood upright again and looked back up the face of the dune, seeing it how it should be seen.

At the very top I could see a
gnarled tree which seemed to have no
leaves or branches. I continued to
climb not because I wanted to see
this dead tree but because of the
tracks which were very odd.

They were animal tracks of three
different kinds but looking to be
one. Dog, horse and bird but all
looking to me as if dog had changed
into horse and then finally a bird. A
bird that seemed to have taken off
from the dune and into the sky.

As I have said there were many
tracks on the island but none of them
were as funny as the ones I found by

the dead tree. And though this tree was no longer living many different grasses grew there, around the base. The grass did not look out of place but the wheels did. Entangled among the grass as if part of the tree was a set of manmade wagon wheels. What it was doing around the tree was as out of the way as the dog, horse and bird tracks.

I stood up and looked down onto the beach.

As the light faded we set long sticks into the shoreline to see how high the tides would come so that we could start building our fish trap the next day.

16

THAT NIGHT we camped at the top of this high dune. It was there that I began making a harness just like the one Wando wore. I made it from dried sea grass washed in along the shore and marram grass which was plenty around the dead tree. I was surprised how strong and pretty it was when rolled together into string.

"I know where the barking dog, lives now," I later said.

"You do?"

"Yes." I answered.

We ate and kept the fire burning bright but soon something else was even brighter. The moon came out. It was round and bright, so round and bright lighting up the whole station and its platforms that we decided to once more go down to the beach and see how blue the moon made the beach look. When we got down it was almost like daytime, except cleaner and more empty.

I stood there for a long time looking down at the bright sands certain something was looking back at us.

I did not know it was a horse but slowly I could tell it was because of the white bit coming out of the sand. Bit by bit this white line got closer and closer till finally I could see a beautiful mustang. The same white mustang we had seen early in the day.

I wished to touch the mustang and so stayed very still. It seemed to take forever but when at last it loomed over me I slowly reached out. I reached out as if trying to touch the moon.

Carefully and in silence, she granted my wish, but not before sniffing at my hand and blowing air onto it. The nose was all white except for the dark patch in between her eyes.

Horses are strong animals. They have firm bodies and a strong smell. With big round, crystal ball eyes that shine and look back at you taking you in like the ocean.

They also take you in by smell, blowing air onto you which was what the white mustang was doing to us, especially at my head because I was so short. Wando was even shorter but she did not mind the sniffing nose and would lick at the horse every time it got close.

But more than anything this giant animal made us feel safe and welcomed.

The horse yawned. It stretched opened its wide horsey mouth that was full of white teeth. Then it yawned again. There was a smell of green grass and beach beet. I brushed my hand down this giant nose and smiled.

"You don't remember, do you?" I whispered. "You are horse now, but once you were like Wando. You lived on the railway. You remember now, don't you?"

She nodded. I brushed. And because this was so much fun Susan also joined in: brushing down the long nodding nose as if it was satisfied. We played this game for some time feeling very safe and secure.

We would see this horse again many times before leaving the island but on the day we left I did not see her and yet, in a funny way much like the horse's snorting and yawning, I did.

"This is where the barking dog lives?" Susan said. "In a horse?"

We laughed about this. We laughed about almost everything about mustangs and dogs and yet at the same time we believed it.

"When the railways closed and the dogs forgotten, they came here and forgot they were dogs and became horses. This is why the white mare and I are friends. She remembers the railway charm. This is also why Wando likes them so much, especially the white one."

Susan did not laugh. She smiled and thought for a while as she always did. She added more sticks to the fire.

"Supposing they are. Why a horse and not pigeon or a cow?"

I too, went quiet and thought for a while.

"I don't know. But I am sure Wando would know." I looked at Wando who was napping nearby and said, "Why do dogs wish to be horses?"

I watched her eye lids move, as if she were dreaming.

17

THE ISLAND was divided into three parts. Beach, dune and grassland. The grassland was where the horses lived most of the time and so did we. The horses must have lived on the island for a long time because every now and then there would be skeletons uncovered by the winds. I don't like skeletons but these horse bones were different. They did not look sad or scary.

We gathered beach beet and collected wild strawberries and cran-berries. Beach beet is a cabbage that grows by the sea. In all the time we spent on the island beach beet was to become our main source of vegetable and the strawberries our vitamin C. We always harvested sea beet at the base leaving the root in which Susan said was good.

We also boiled seawater to make salt. The sea is made of salt the same way tears are made of salt and yet it still felt strange to see white crystals appear in the pot after boiling.

We left the last of the roots cooking in the embers and returned to the fish trap. This we broadly made by jabbing many long sticks into the sand. Seen from above it was like the shape of an arrow, with the tip acting as a net. How it worked is like this: as the tide came in the fish would follow the arrow shaft and then into the net which we made out of many different things like rubbish and beach vine. To complete the job I think we must have gathered almost every long stick along the shore.

It was late afternoon when we got back to camp. The roots were cooked nicely and had a crispy skin. I broke the first one into two. The aroma was so good that it made Wando twitch her nose.

I made a small collection of beach things and took a photo. In it were crab shells and sea beans, some I took back to Joan Island.

We spent much time digging for clams. This was the part I liked best because digging is fun and you never know what you might find. And besides, clams are very good eating, whichever way you cook them.

I really liked the sweat bees. They were much smaller than common bees and did not make honey and did not sting us. Instead they liked sweat.

We ran out of soap and so began using beach vine which lathers up just like soap.

We found a ball and with it played a short game of volleyball.

At dusk we went back to check on the fish trap. The tide was not fully out but we wanted to get there before the gulls did. The first fish we caught turned out to be our biggest. A flat fish called flounder. The other two fish had nice markings but we let them go because they were too small. We never again caught another fish as big as that first one.

There were special birds that flew across the sea. They flew so low and fast they looked to me as if they were skiing. The small ones always flew in numbers of threes and fours while the larger ones flew alone. And because I had the spyglass I could clearly see their beaks dipped into the water as they flew which was very clever. During these times there was no difference between the sea and the sky. It was the same.

The pool was a good place to see the swimming birds. I liked the ducks taking off and landing. I especially liked the petrels turning in their circles which we could watch all day long.

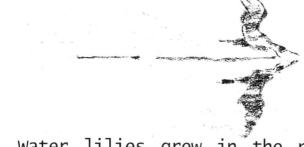

Water lilies grew in the pond and Susan did think about gathering some.
"We could eat the bulbs and the seeds,"
But we never did this because of what I saw.
It looked like a bird on water. But there was no head. The tail was going bottoms up yet it stayed that way for a long time so it could not have been a bird for it did not come up for air.
I pointed this to Susan and she said it might have been a fish.
"It's probably got the bird and trying to drown it."
"A fish catching a bird?"
Susan gave me a nod. "Who knows what lives in that pond?"
Sometimes the ponds got quite noisy because of the birds. The most noisy times was when the gulls came. They would circle and circle making ugly

cac-cac-cac noises as if telling others they had found food. Terns are small birds and it was fun to see them chase off their bigger enemy by picking and pulling at their tails. They are brave birds and we helped them whenever we could by throwing sticks and stones at the gulls.

Perhaps the terns were protecting their eggs.

We had seen cranes fly by a number of times and one day, followed them. They seemed to be always going to a western part of the island and we wondered why. When we got there and they fled, it seemed they had been digging in a patch of star sedge. Probably after the seeds there that were quite numerous.

Bird sounds are nice. But they don't make you fall asleep the way grasshoppers do.

Dune grasshoppers are not that big. They are sand in colour but I did see some green ones. I spent much time listening and watching grasshoppers. Their world is small and dry and is always made of grass. The song they make is done by rubbing their wings against their legs. It's a sound that always makes you nice and sleepy and a lot of the times I did.

Henry, like Wando, also stayed by the horses. There he attacked anything that moved under the horse's feet. Lizards, beetles and horseflies but he did not bother with lady birds which were quite big.

I suppose sand meant something else to a bird, especially to one who liked to scratch and dig.

Henry dug at the sand. He even took sand baths by flicking the sand over himself. He dug at it all day long. Even Wando joined in. She would dig and sniff at the grass roots as if trying to sniff out another world.

It was all very funny and we laughed, but our laughter turned to surprise when Henry began finding grubs. There was bird food living in the sand! These grubs lived under a low growing bush and were white with a black hardened head. I do not know if this helped but a few times we dug this grub ourselves and tossed them into the fish trap hoping it might lure in more fish.

A few times while digging we found sea shells at the base of a dune which were burnt as if someone had cooked and ate them long ago. But the strangest one was a round stone that had a channel running through the middle.

It did not mean much to me but Susan said she would like to have it.

"If you give me that, I will give you this,"

I looked. She held it up with both hands like a sports trophy, which it was!

"Probably left over from days of the railway," she said. She brushed off the sand and began reading what was written on it.

"This trophy is awarded to Joan of Heart, the maker of magic circles..."

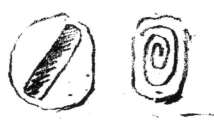

I found a dream stone. It was among the seaweed on the beach when the tide was out. When I picked it up I knew right away what it was. I could not see what else it could have been.

The markings on it swirled and swirled in the way of dreams.

We caught octopus! It was eating a crab in the trap and so was caught. It was not big but it made a good meal. Octopus is not like anything else in the sea. There is no bone and no shape. The suckers feel very strange when it latches onto you. But it works poorly on animals such as a dog or chicken.

We boiled the octopus for soup. The crab was good also. With this we each had a claw. It was all very tasty!

We are people who cook in silence and Susan did the same. She never hit the pans nor knocked spoons. This I know Grandmother would have liked because it is considered bad manners to hit a pan.

There are no long, wide beaches on Joan Island. The sand there, in some parts is harsh and gritty.

The sand on Diana was soft and fine, especially in the far west where the island ends. Here it entered the sea like a spear.

I knelt down and touched the water. The sea on our left was warm but the sea to our right was cool. The cool side was were most of the crabs preferred to live. Ghost crabs they are called.

Roosters don't lay eggs but on the way back we found some across the heath. They were spotted but larger than most. I think they were gulls eggs.

It was good that we found eggs because we did not catch any fish. The only thing in the fish trap was a very thin clam. It was large, almost round but was very thin.

"I have seen this before," Susan told me. "It is very good eating."

"You have it," I said. "You are older."

I said this because there was hardly any meat. But in the end we shared, cutting it in half like a biscuit.

We went looking for more the next day but this meant having to wade into the shallows. I was fearful because of sharks.

"I won't go far," she promised.

It was late in the afternoon and the tide was heading out. I watched Susan standing out of the water which was up to her chest. But she would disappear whenever she bent down to feel for the clams.

I was stood in the water, too. I held onto Wando while scanning the deep sea. I was looking for sharks when, suddenly I thought I saw one. A fin rose out of the water and swiftly went back in.

My heart jumped. But then I became calm again. I knew it was a dolphin. Only dolphins swim up for air like a hump.

Later I told Susan what I saw and she said it was a good omen for she had found a fair number of this thin good tasting clam and more.

I wanted to pick a blue thing that came out of the surf but Susan stopped me.

"They sting," she said.

I suppose the biggest difference, besides the crabs which did not make balls but instead scavenged like the gulls, was sound.

Joan Island is rocky and the waves pounded the rocks. Here there were no rocks and the surf was smooth and on some days, flat and calm. And if you got behind a dune you would not think you are on an island at all.

Horses have the best hearing. Even from afar they could pick up the music from my radio. I know they could because they would stop among the dune grass and look my way not moving for a long time. The colts, or baby horses, they especially liked my radio and would follow me around making their sweet braying noises of which I heard often.

Not all the horses ran away. We spotted one horse with a long rope around its neck and because of this it could neither walk well nor run fast because the rope was like an unwanted long tail that got in the way.

"The poor thing..." I said. "Can't we do something?"

We did try thinking of different ways but the only one we could think of was to get close and cut the rope with the sickle and make it shorter. But in the end what happened was the horse spooked and I was dragged along with it.

It pulled me a good distance along the wet beach before finally letting go.

When I again opened my eyes I saw Susan. She was wiping the sand off my face.

"Joan? Are you hurt? Answer me?"

But all I did was laugh. I let go of the rope and put up my horsey hands that was very waxy from touching the horse and laughed.

Since we felt we were the only people on the island we did not wonder why or how the rope got around the horse's neck. So much people's rubbish had washed in along the shore that we did not think it out of place.

"I really like this," I said.

"What do you mean?"

"This. I really like being here with you. Just us, Wando, Henry, you and me. It's really good fun."

Susan looked away and thought for a moment. Then she looked back.

"You care about Wando. Much more than anyone else on the island and you don't even live here. May I ask why?"

At first my answer was simple. "I had a scary dream..."

But then I thought of a better reason.

"Wando wanted to go into this old house but I did not like it. I went and carried her out but on the way out I was caught by barb wire. I was holding onto Wando while the barb was holding onto me. But somehow Wando raised her legs as if she was kicking the barb and I was free. It was as if she knew what to do, as if she were really helping me. Perhaps this is the real reason why I love her so much."

The sun shone everyday on the island
of Diana and soon the small ponds
began to dry. This was good for the
terns for they pecked off the last of
the small fish. But the smallest and
shallowest pond of them all, which
lay west, specks of tiny flashes were
dying and baking under the sun for
they had flopped out of the drying
ponds only to find themselves in one
even hotter frying pan.

"This place," Susan said, "Is what
Joan Island feels like in October.
The air is cool, but not sticky. It's
so nice to sit by the sea and watch
the sun go down. Yet this good
weather does not last."

18

THE ISLAND of Diana was a happy place and we did not want to leave. The fishing was easy and there was no one else but us and the horses swinging their lazy tails. But in the end we had to leave.

As I have said, there were many footprints along the beach. Birds, crabs, horses, worms and beetles. But the footprint of man was different. This was the thing that made us go home.

We found it on the day we came back to the island. We had been away for about half a day heading north east as opposed to going home. We wanted to see how far the railway went, which seemed to me, went on forever.

It probably did. But we could not tell. There was a large gate stopping us from going any further. It was high above the water meaning that we could see a wooded place not far from us but could not get close.

I remember standing outside this giant gate squinting for the sun was high.

"I have never seen a gate in the middle of the ocean before," I said. "Perhaps there is a key?"

We did try looking for one, but around this gate, apart from the hanging creepers, it was as bare as the ocean and we found nothing.

"Whatever it is," Susan finally said, "I am sure this gate is not to keep us out but to keep something in."

I took out my camera and snapped a photo. I framed it so that I was looking over Wando's big ears that were peering through the gate and into a mysterious forbidden place.

We did not stay long because the sun was bearing down on us and there was no shade.

Since we had not seen the east part of Diana island, only the west, we decided to go and have a look once we got back and we did. On the way out that morning we had seen something that surprised us greatly. A patch of bright red. All over the island the dominant colour was green but, east of the island it was bright red.

The railway was a disappointment but the island, this we could at the least go and find out.

We kept to the beach at first. The sand was hard and easier to walk on. It was only when we felt we were close did we move onto the dunes. The first thing we found was the footprint.

I remember the first time I found the tracks of boars. I immediately took precautions and blocked off the mouth of Bride's Cave. The boars came looking for something to eat. But what did man come for?

Not far away we found the reason.

A poppy field.

I like poppies. They are pretty and bright but there was something very wrong.

At the edge of the field, hanging over the wooden posts like a gateway was a dead dog. Its jaws were agape and dried skin was still attached to the skull. It was horrible.

Susan took a step forward but I did not move. All I could think of was the dead dog but what Susan thought about was not the same.

"*Where the poppies grow nobody goes,*" she said, as if singing.

I did not want to go into this spooky field but I wanted to understand what Susan meant, because under the dead dog were chicken claws and black stained knives which made me feel very uncomfortable.

I walked to where she stood and took hold of her hand. She looked down at me.

"Dearest Joan, don't be frightened. These are not wild poppies. Someone planted the seeds and watered them when there was no rain. This dead dog is meant to be a warning."

"They are bad people?"

She nodded.

"Yes. They are somewhere. But we cannot see them..."

I looked. But still the island stood empty both to the east and the west. I was scared now, but I was also very angry. All I could think of was the poor dog.

I raised the sword intending to strike down a row of poppies. But I did not bring down the blade. I was too upset.

We cleared the tracks we made in the sand so that no one would know we had been there and walked back along the shore. I was still very upset and said nothing but with Wando trotting at my heels looking as if she knew I was upset and Susan saying, "You walk like a boy..." I could not stay silent for long.

It was then that I felt I could say something that I have wanted to say for some time.

"Grandmother said you are to marry soon."

She looked at me very surprised.

"She did?"

"Yes. She said when you marry you have to pay the man and I asked why and she said it was dowry. She said this is why you work so hard, to save up and get married."

I kept my gaze on Susan hoping that Grandmother was wrong and when at last she slowly began to laugh, I felt much better.

"I'd much rather marry a horse! Wouldn't you?"

She ran from me egging me to catch her and I did. In the end we both went rolling in the sand where finally Wando got the chance to lick at my face.

I did not like wet things against my cheeks and so I shrieked.

"*ERRH!*" I shouted, pushing away the wet and soggy nose and a tongue which I thought smelt a lot like fish.

I thought that night was to be our last night on the island. Since there clearly was no dog alive on the island except mustangs and now, the cruel fields of poppies I could see no point in staying.

"Are we going home now?"

But she shook her head.

"But you said it's dangerous to stay?"

"It is dangerous,"

I looked. I did not understand.

"Do you remember what you said to the man who chained dogs?"

"Do you mean: *How would you like it if you were tied up like that? With no place to run and no water to wash yourself?*"

It was not meant to be funny but it was because we both said the lines at the same time which made it funny.

"We are going home," she said at last. "But first we must make some arrows."

She did not say what the arrows were for and I did not ask.

Inside Diana station there were lots of old things like barrels and containers. These barrels were mostly empty and broken but there were some that had oil and paraffin which at one time was probably used to light the lighthouse and the many lamps around the station.

We spent the next morning scraping out something that was neither and laid it across the platform to dry. It had an awful smell to it.

Again I did not ask what it was, for this would spoil the fun.

We left the mud to dry under the hot sun and went searching for sticks that could be made into arrows. As we walked the beach I asked Susan did she dream and she said no. Then she asked if I did and I said yes.

"It was very strange and scary," I said.

"Oh?"

"There were masks."

"Masks?"

"Yes. Many, many masks. They were very scary to look at."

"Scary masks?"

"Yes. They were rolling and burning down a hill going *woooohooooo!* just like a steam train. But also there was the sound of running animals, like a stampede."

"A stampede?"

I nodded.

"Masks, fire, hill, steam train and stampede."

I watched her count each of the things I spoke of using her fingers. After which she held out all five fingers saying, "That is a strong dream, Joan. Very strong..."

Perhaps it was because of my strong dreaming that made us gather wood to make a big bonfire.

We built it on top of the tallest dune around the dead tree. This was fun to do but the one I liked best was trying to find driftwood that was long and straight enough to make an arrow. Because when we did find enough to make three (straight sticks being very hard to come by along the beach) I finally got to see what the stone with the channel running down the middle was for. It was to sand and straighten the shaft of an arrow, especially after they had been softened through the fire.

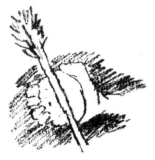

By the time we got back to Diana station the bad smelling mud had dried itself into a thick, heavy powder. It was then that I could see and understand what we had been drying.

Gunpowder.

My mouth fell open.

"I know how they work," Susan said, meaning the cannons. "We have two back on the island. At weekends we used to make them fire but nowadays that is done no more."

I did not know anything about cannons but to make them bang I was told we had to make bags and the only material we had were our skirts.

At first I was not so happy about destroying my Scout uniform. But since my skirt was already torn and the odour of white smoke was strong from lighting so many camp fires, I agreed.

Afterwards I took a photo of Susan, saying, "So you know what you looked like!"

And she, in return did the same. "So you know what *you* looked like!"

But what we really did look like were two ragged looking girls who had been living on a deserted island where everyday we fished and foraged for a living.

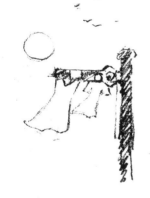

As the sun dipped low across the sea we filled each of the three bags with gunpowder. There was plenty of powder but not enough fabric to make the bags.

The cannon balls were next. They lay below our feet. They were stacked like a small pyramid next to the grass covered cannon. We lifted one of these and put it in the cannon facing south, on top of the bag of gunpowder. They were big and heavy. Then Susan went to the other end of the cannon where there was a hole, almost like a flute hole. There, with a sharp stick she pushed down and poured in more powder.

"Do you think I should hold both my ears?" I asked.

"You may," she answered. "When the time comes,"

We did not know when this time would be but looking down onto the wide and darkening beach where the cannon nose was pointing, I had a strange feeling that it would not be long.

19

THE POPPY pirates came on a sunless day. They came on speedboats and sped along the shore on motorbikes.

I spied their movements from behind a dune. Two rode very noisy motorbikes while another two, walked up from behind. I was not so frightened because we had been waiting for them.

They were heading west, the part of the island where we made camp.

I did not know what their intentions were but it did not take long for me to find out. A group of mustangs were nearby and the motorbikes were chasing them along the beach. I could see they carried a long pole at the end of which was a noose.

Now I knew why the horses did not like us. They were afraid we might do the same.

Quickly I ran back passed the dunes while staying out of sight.

Already Susan was crouched behind a low dune, her arrows ready.

She was lighting each one when I came to and said, "They're stealing our horses!"

By now the pirates were very close, so close that we could hear them talk as we lay silently behind the dunes. It was a language I have never heard of and one Susan could barely understand.

The arrows were sticking out of the sand. They looked like burning candles because around the tip we had wrapped bits of our skirts. They also burnt well because of the paraffin and whale oil.

I knew the bonfire would distract the pirates because they did not know about us. And while they looked one way, we run the other, back to Diana station unseen. But lighting the bon fire was the hard part. It was too far to climb up the dune but to shoot the arrow meant having to stand up and risk the chance of being seen. But it was a chance we had to take.

Carefully I peeked over the dune. The pirates were closer than ever but they were too busy trying to restrain a horse.

Now was a good time to send the arrow.

"*Clear!*" I said.

The arrow went into the sky and quickly Susan was back on her knees. We waited. But nothing happened, or not much.

The bonfire wood was quite far and I wondered whether it was too far to make a good target.

A second arrow was fired. And then a third, meaning the last and still nothing happened. And then Henry crowed.

Roosters crow all day long. And here, in a place with no other chickens to talk to, Henry perhaps wanting chicken talk, crowed more than ever.

At that instance I could see in my mind the pirates looking our way. Quickly I put my hand over his beak.

Not long after this came the sound of horses. It sounded very close and seemed very angry. Carefully I again peeked over. It was a horse.

And it was very angry for it was kicking out its front legs at the pirates who looked to be afraid.

Now was chance. Quickly we scrambled back through the dunes and made our way up to where the canons stood.

The bonfire did burn after all. Looking back I could see it burning high engulfing the dead tree. But there were other fires that should not have been there which surprised me greatly. It was moving along the beach in a strange way. That was when I spied through the spyglass and saw the wheels. The wheels that once sat on top of the tall dune were now at the bottom and rolling down the beach, but on fire! I tried to see where the pirates were but there was no time for this.

As I have said, the gun was old and we had no idea if it worked.

The first shot made a great thunder in the air. I held my ears and hoped that perhaps by some chance it might land on their motorbikes. It did not.

Instead it hit the water and made a big splash which we could see.

The second cannon ball also went into the sea but did something we did not expect. It pushed the whole cannon back towards us and landed with a loud crash on the tracks. A good thing no one was standing behind it at the time.

This cannon was useless now. Time to go and use the other. But on the way over I carelessly dropped the powder which made the bag burst. It spilled out like black sand next to a strange vase with figure head.

Fortunately I had with me the agave needle, the one I harvested which I planned to use on my skirt but did not. Quickly I took it out from my neck purse and began working on the tear. Since there was already a thread attached I did not have to waste time putting one on so my work was fast.

By the time I was done Susan, with great effort had turned the cannon around. It now faced the island instead of the ocean.

As I pushed in the gunpowder I could almost see the pirates fleeing in their boats and taking their bikes with them.

I held my ears. The platform shuddered once more. Then silence.

We crossed over to the other side of the tracks and looked down.

The pirates had gone. There was no sign of them anywhere. We and the horses were safe. The beach was once again empty.

Now it was our turn for we too were
leaving. We went back down to the
beach to collect a few of our things
and also to pick some wild
strawberries.

The last of the sun made tall
shadows across blades of grass which
flickered from time to time. The way
they turned gold was like a magic
lantern show.

I was standing not far from the big
dune and wondering about the white
horse when I looked up and saw what I
thought was part of the lantern show.
The dead tree at the top was still
standing but now it did not look dead
anymore. It was like a giant hand
with smoke coming from it. A hand as
if waving and saying hello. And next

to this was something I had never seen.

I picked up my spyglass and what I saw instantly made my heart beat fast. It was a dog! A big one, and white, sitting next to the big smoking hand!

I dropped everything and ran hoping I would get there in time and find another dog. Wando also ran and soon overtook me. But when I got to the top both of the dogs had gone. They were running away across the beach looking like one was chasing the other.

With my heart still beating fast I hurried back to Susan with the news.

She too was picking wild strawberries but when I told her what I saw the strawberries fell to the ground.

I too had dropped my strawberries when I saw what I saw but I did not fall to my knees and begin to cry as Susan did, especially after I refused to leave the island.

"Those pirates will return and when they find out we are just two girls, a dog and a rooster they will not think it funny. We have to leave!"

But still I shook my head. "No..."

Perhaps it was because I was stubborn. Or perhaps it was the loud thunder made by cannons which shook the ground beneath us. It may even have been the sea because when you cry it is salty, like the sea. It may also have been the number sixteen which was how old Susan was. Sixteen being the age you worry and Susan did worry. Whatever it was, it was too much and she was upset.

I was shocked. It was the first time I have ever seen her cry. I felt bad she was unhappy but I could not bring myself to leave, not just yet.

I picked up the strawberries and put them back in her hand.

"I love you, Susan." I slowly said.

At last she took off her glasses and looked up.

"I love you, too!" she replied.

Then I said, "More than you will love a man?"

This I knew would make her happy and it did.

She put her arms around me and gave me a big cuddle. The strawberries were crushed but it did not seem to matter.

"Now we are even," I said. "I burst into tears once. And now, you too. We really are sisters!"

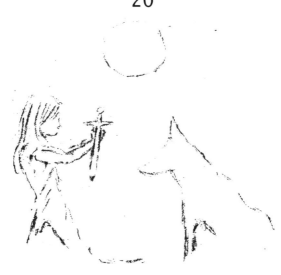

20

WANDO had not returned so we had no choice but to stay another night. We camped out this last night on the same tall dune which I now named "The Place of Hallo". I left the railway charm sticking out of the sand both for protection and to attract the dogs.

We also left out enough food for Wando and the new dog should they return.

When we finished I asked Susan, "Why do we scream when we are afraid?" and she replied,

"I don't know," but then she went on to say, "why do lions *roar* and ducks *qwack*?"

"You mean screaming is good?"

"I think so, don't you?"

I said, "Yes," And then stumbling a little I said, "I think we scream because we are trying to frighten away what is scaring us. This tells others how strong we are."

Susan laughed, saying I was probably right. "We need help sometimes and we need to tell others we need help. Even if it is just being afraid,"

I suppose I should have been afraid but strangely I was not. I slept soundly and did not dream.

In the morning the first thing I did was to go and look at the food we left out the night before. The bowl was empty.

The sun had just risen. I looked down across the beach and saw big waves crashing in. The voice of the sea was busy and noisy, but it did not stop me from picking up my spyglass and seeing two dogs running with joy in their hearts. They ran slowly, jogging up their heads and tails like the waves of the ocean.

I grab the charm and quickly made my way down to the beach. The new dog was white and much taller and ran with grace just like a horse. When they saw me they both came trotting my way as if they had never been away.

At first I did not touch the new dog but soon she came close and sat down looking at me. She was breathing through a big smiling mouth that was also yawning wide like a horse. I put my hand out and she let me touch her. Her coat was thick but soft.

"You have changed back!" I spoke at last. "The last time I saw you, you were a horse. Now you are a dog!"

I tied the harness I made across her chest making sure it was not too tight.

I then raised the shimmering sword saying, "I think this is yours," I rested it carefully on to her back and tied a bow knot around it which she did not seemed to mind.

I stayed like that for some time admiring my work and the way the sun was gleaming across the metal.

I had not thought the white dog would return with us to Joan Island. Finding her was wonderful but to have her come back with us was a wish I did not make but overjoyed when it happened. It happened because of Wando. The two dogs were the best of friends, like sisters.

I did not question how or why because when you dream happy you do not think of such things.

We began to pack and was soon ready to leave.

The morning was bright but to the east stood banks of grey clouds which probably meant a storm was coming so there was no time to lose.

As the five of us started back towards the station the sound of the waves crashing ashore grew louder. The winds hummed and the tall grass swayed wildly. In all the time we stayed on the island it was quiet and nothing moved but now I felt uneasy, as if at any moment a pirate might appear because it was hard to hear their approach.

But what really happened was very funny.

As I came to the top of the stairs a huge nose and head came out of nowhere and looked down at me.

It was a cow, and not just one but the whole herd!

I gasped, but did not scream.

"They must have followed us," I heard Susan say. She was smiling at the big horned head looking down at me which made me understand that this was another good omen.

With so many new friends at our side no pirates would dare come near us! We were now very safe.

"They have come to see us off!" Susan cried.

The cows stood around the platform and the tracks as if they were waiting for a train. But really, as

Susan had said, they had come to say goodbye.

It was good that the cows came for they were guardians of the old railway. It is they who have kept the railway open by eating back the trees and grass and keeping it tidy. But their horns were big and their bodies even bigger, how were we to get passed them? If only I had a whistle I could have blown it to move them out of the way but then one of our dogs began to bark.

She barked loud, as only a big dog can and it echoed strongly against the station walls. I liked this hollow sound because it sounded like talking rather than barking. I liked it even more when the cows began to clear a path for us. This put a big smile on my face and I decided there and then to name her "Joansun" which can mean one of two things: Spirit Helper or Joan's Dog.

Joan's Dog kept on talking to the cows and the cows in return kept shuffling and galloping down the tracks as if they were a train that could not be stopped.

We waved goodbye to the cows who along with Diana station were soon far behind us. I shouted, "Thank you for a lovely time!" but all they did was look at me and become smaller and

smaller till they could barely be
seen except for the dark clouds that
seemed to be chasing us.

21

ALL THE TIME we thought the storm was coming from behind us, to the north. But we soon saw that it was coming in from the east, which was to our left.

At first all I could think of was the wind. That it might blow us off the trestle or carry away the animals who had nothing to hold onto as we did. I knew the winds were growing strong because it made the storm house ring with all its might. We passed under one and I could feel its thunder. The sound was as frightening as it was wonderful.

We never thought the valleys and channels which the track ran through would become a torrent and flood, it did.

When the rain came it was very heavy and fast. Swirls of water thrashed around us wetting us even more. For some time we could see no metal track for the water had covered it. Yet we kept going and did not stop.

But very quickly we had to abandon ship for the cart had become one. Water rose around it as we clambered up the slippery valley.

We watched helpless as the cart was overcome. It vanished under water then surfaced again half in, half out. In the end it ended up caught within a bush.

We climbed as high as we could go and stayed under a huge rock. The rain was very cold now and I began to shiver but fortunately we had the animals with us. We clung onto them for warmth. I, to Wando. And Susan, to Joansun. Henry also clung to us, burying his head under his red cloak and standing on one leg as if sleeping.

I remember when Joan station was flooded and I was afraid but now I was very afraid. Things were being washed down by raging water. The largest being a tree. As it passed by it nudged the cart free which made Susan and the big dog go back in. Together they were quickly caught in the current. In all the time we had been away this was the time I felt most afraid.

But the rain did not last. Gradually the water began to ease and in doing so began to drain fast. I pulled Susan back under the rock and together we watched the rush below turn steady till we could almost see the line of the railway reappear.

The cart had not been washed away. It was now wedged further down behind a different bush, one that was in blossom. We climbed down and freed it from the branches so that it could roll down onto the watery tracks with a splash.

We were still cold but after wringing out the rain from our clothes and getting started we felt better and began to get warm. It was good that we moved off because this meant we were also moving away from the rains. Soon the frogs began singing and the sun came out. It now felt like a new day.

We pushed on and in no time were passing island after island as if the railway was a string and we were rewinding ourselves. The air was hot and sticky and once more it was summertime. We had traveled from the cold of the storm and made it back to summer. But summer was already ending on the railway.

Red seeds fell out of the sky. They looked like a shower of red butterflies. A bone also fell. We wondered what had dropped it but all there was in the sky were black birds. Perhaps they were ravens.

I did not think we would reach home within the same day but at dusk the outline of Joan Island appeared on the horizon and once more we were plunged into the blackness of Bride's Cave. Except this time it did not last long and the feeling was very different.

BOOK III

Joansun

22

I WAS HAPPY to be back. And though I was very tired, I felt very satisfied. Much more than I would have been had I traveled by motor car or boat.

But the scariest part turned out to be coming home itself. When we came out of the tunnel thinking we were safe, the small stream that normally lay far below us under the bridge was foaming with the rage of the ocean. It was making white water above the bridge and licking the air. We paid no attention to the animals before but now we had to. We worried whether the current would wash them away and down the cliff. That was when we found out there was no brake because we never needed to use them.

"Jump!" Susan cried and took hold of Henry by the wings. At that moment all I could hear was Henry's protest at being suddenly flung and the changing sound of the wheels as we approached the platform.

we had to jump because the tracks ran into thick brambles and wild roses that were full of thorns.

The big dog and Susan went first but by the time Wando jumped the platform had passed me by. It was now too late for me to jump.

A low branch was hanging above the railway and quickly, without thinking I took hold of it with both hands. As the empty cart speeded on I was left dangling.

I watched the cart enter the thorns and come to a sudden silent stop. I let go and landed bending both my legs as I did so. Slowly I turned my head and looked back at the station.

It was all very quiet, as if waiting for something. It was so quiet that I wondered where all the birds had gone. We had been gone that long a wasp had made its tiny nest under the arch. It was beautifully crafted, almost like honeycombs but different.

We cooked and fed the animals and it was decided that I would stay at the station while Susan left to go home making sure my grandparents knew I was safe and all was well.

I do not remember what I dreamt of that night but in the morning I found two dogs sleeping under me.

From that day on I felt the station, the dogs and I were one. Rather than feeling I should not be here, I felt it was wrong the place be left abandoned and unkept. So began the task of bringing the station back to life. I knew things would never be the same again. The trains and passengers will never return. But someone did live here and now more than one so it did deserve to look like a place of the living.

The first place we began to uncover was the signal box. This was another part of the station I was curious about for a long time. It was hidden behind tall and heavy undergrowth and the staircase could not be reached so was probably one of the first places to be abandoned.

There were two tracks beside the platform. One was the main track and the other, a waiting track, meaning one train could be parked to one side while the other passed it. The signal box was there to divert the parked train in and out of track two with the use of several long levers.

We hacked at the creepers and branches around the staircase till at last sunlight could enter the wooden floors and light up the many handles and switches that one time operated the tracks.

Much of the glass in the windows had broken. Probably by the heat and the growing branches. But our biggest surprise was that it was not locked. I turned the brass handle and walked in.

At first the room smelled damp but we soon cleaned the wooden floor and it began to feel cozy.

I liked the higher view from there because you could just about see Bride's Cave. Also, there were lots of windows. And things always look and feel different because there are.

We then planted flowers in the many empty flower pots and put them along the platform.

I took a photo afterwards and placed it next to a photo of the station when I first arrived. The station before I came and the station that is now, because we came.

"It all seems so friendly now," I said. "Bride's Cave looks just like a big dog house. Don't you think?"

Susan looked at me and smiled. She was wearing a flower in her hair and I did too.

As I have said, there were jumbled things growing around the station that attracted the wild hogs to come and dig. I knew the cucumbers were good but the cabbages, fruits and roots growing in strange jumbled ways that were food to hogs I had not tried. But one evening after Joansun had bravely chased them off, barking down into Bride's Cave so loud I was sure whatever great evil there was would surely have left like the giant pigs, we went and tried this food for ourselves. I knew that pigs can stomach what we cannot but the roots we roasted were delicious. And the wild cabbage was really a kale.

"This must be a magic garden," I said. "There are no shovels nor rakes and no one to sow seeds and yet there is food."

"Yes dear," Susan answered. "It is like a forest of wild food. The vegetables grown next to fruits and they are mixed and jumbled but they are fruits and vegetables you can eat!"

The last place to be cleaned was the entrance. This I saved for the last. I liked this part best because it meant I did not have to bend down under the thorns when coming and going out of the station. I sang while cutting back the nettles and when it was done, was surprised to find plant pots flanked along each side of the entrance.

It felt good to at last be able to come through the gate and see a path and to be able to walk down it without the thorns and darkness.

I knew that clearing the entrance would attract attention, but the work satisfied me and left me feeling very happy.

"The beautiful station named Joan!" I declared.

I closed the gate and locked it. Then, with the two dogs trotting at our heels went down to the water front singing all the way.

23

THERE ARE many different keys in the world. Some are made of steel and can lock and unlock gates and doors. But there are keys that live and talk. They too lock and unlock gates and doors, but of a different kind.

I remember the day Wando got her voice back. It was sad and happy at the same time. Happy, not because Wando really got her voice back. It was because her future was dark no more.

The two dogs were standing side by side and the big one was barking at the main gate. And behind the gate, as if frightened was the Saw Man. The sight of him once again made me unhappy, even though he was standing on the other side of the gate. And though the dogs were keeping him out, I knew this would not be forever.

It was Grandfather. My grandfather was the key. In the end he was the one who kept Saw Man out for good and not the dogs.

"*Grandfather!*" I shouted.

He looked at me through the gate and slowly opened his mouth, showing his two missing front teeth.

"*Oyyhh!*" he answered, which was how he always answered me. Like a slow fog horn.

I knew very little about Grandfather. Before I was born he had been a carpenter making boats that went fishing out at sea but stopped this after the boats became steel. I knew that he liked to read everyday after work, on the veranda facing the sea. "Kung fu novels," Grandmother called them. But now all of a sudden I felt as if I knew him very well.

Grandfather's key was memory. And how long he had lived. Grandfather was older then the Saw Man. I know this because the Saw Man called him "Bune Sook," which means: Uncle Bune. This is quite funny because Bune Sook can also sound like "half baked". The Saw Man bowed to "half baked" and took off his hat. And in return "half baked" did the same.

"This is my Granddaughter," he told him proudly. He was not a talking man my Grandfather probably because he spoke with a terrible stutter but not today.

The Saw Man looked at me and then at Grandfather. But instead of looking stern he nodded slowly and soon left, saying he was busy. Again he took off his hat and Grandfather did likewise.

"Saw" which means: lock, can also mean: silly or mad.

From that day on he never again came to Joan station and neither did the wild pigs. It was as if the two dogs together were really keeping them away.

"This is good place," said Grandfather.

"But how did you know I was here?" I asked.

"I have followed you many times," he answered. "You are my grand-daughter and this place, no one comes no more. You see that tower? It was made by your Great Aunty,"

"Yes I know," I replied.

I showed him the bright sword. The one I found up the tree.

He grinned, saying, "You are my granddaughter. You are meant to find it."

I held his big old hands which were very wrinkly and told him everything. How I made a bow and scaled the tower. And how we then went into the tunnel and found a faraway island.

To all of this, he smiled saying, "*Heremere?*" which means something like is that right? He was especially pleased with the new basket I had made, since after all, making things in wood was what he did best.

"I found her, too," I said, pointing to the big white animal who was carrying the bright blade.

He would look at the dog wide eyed, and once more smiled showing his two missing front teeth. I never thought that Grandfather would be the one. The one key which finally opened the station for good but it was.

Grandfather would return many times before the summer was over and together we would walk the beach looking for things. He even returned to me the old key, the one that was taken from me but on the day I went to tell him I was leaving he turned from me and walked into the veranda saying nothing. Probably to read his kung fu books.

"Never mind him!" Grandmother said, consoling me. "He is like that. It upsets him that you are leaving."

It is hard to leave a place, I know. And even harder when you are left behind.

We spent many happy days together, the dogs and I, exploring not only the beach but the empty houses with no doors. Such places I would have thought frightening had Joansun not been at my side.

From the beginning I have always known and felt her stay was to be short because the station was not her home and, because she was beginning to remember. I had heard her grunting in her sleep which sounded to me very much like a horse.

I remember the day before she left. We were down by the water front where the children would come and look at the dogs. Most of the girls and boys were happy with touching the dogs but there was one boy who wanted more.

He tried taking the sword away but Joansun turned and bared her teeth. She was a big dog anyway and the growl she made was threatening. Quickly the boy back off, looking scared.

I stepped forward. I knew I could take the sword because I was the one who put it there.

I held up the charm for all to see. The blade blended strangely with the sky and seemed to almost disappear.

That night I took off both dog harness to wash and left them out to dry. This meant they were now free of their burdens.

I even said to her, "Don't go! This does not mean you can go back to being a horse!"

But the next morning when I returned she was gone. The platform was empty.

I found Wando on the beach looking up at the sky, at a flock of birds heading east but there was no sign of the other dog.

I always knew she would leave one day but felt bad we did not have a proper goodbye. I stood at the mouth of Bride's Cave calling for sometime but never again did I hear the voice of a barking dog.

"Perhaps this is why we cannot bring things back from a dream," I said to Wando who was watching the wind in the leaves. All over the station was quiet and nothing moved. No leaves nor branches and yet here the leaves moved like nowhere else.

24

I REMEMBER those last days of summer like a dream. A dream where I would wake and the sun shone on the beach and I would go there and look for footprints in the sand. It feels like a dream now and yet it was no dream.

Everyday the dogs ran along the beach. And everyday they picked up things in their mouths swinging and running with it in a very playful way. A running that was like skipping, as if there really was a rope under their feet.

Susan never again spoke of Wando's future and I never asked. After having seen how bright it was on the other side of Bride's Cave, I now felt different. And though Wando went back to being her old self, staring and waiting at the mouth of Bride's Cave I knew this was no longer foolish.

"You are going to be lonely now," I said.

I suppose in a way she was and yet she was not.

One day we heard a cat's meow. It came loud from within Bride's Cave and it did this without pause as if she were singing. When at last she came out, a thing that was black and white, she meowed as if she was talking to us.

The cat was dangerous. I say this because I was struck many times. She had claws sharp as a knife and when struck, I did not bleed right away but later. She never stayed long and did not liked to stay long and in time I learnt not to get in her way but somehow she soon became Wando's friend.

I guess when you are alone, even a fierce cat is good company.

This fierce nature I felt was good for Wando because she was not fierce. A good train station needs a cat, and a dog. A cat to sleep in the chair and a dog to watch on the platforms. This meant she now had someone who could defend and perhaps even look out for her.

"Don't worry, Wando. I will return soon. I won't leave you. In the meantime you have Susan, and your new cat friend. And what a friend she is! She is fierce but funny. Have you seen how she rolls across the floor, frolicking as if she wants you to play? Have you seen how she can jump and fly over my head then over the wall? You have nothing to fear!"

25

THE DAYS went fast for Wando and me and soon it was time for me to leave. On my last day I went back to the station and again climbed the tree. I climbed and put back the railway charm. The charm that looks like a sword but is not a sword at all.

I stood on the tracks one more time and looked around myself, listening to the air rush by and the birds sing.

I closed my eyes and breathed in.

"Goodbye," I said.

I picked up my bags and left.

The Ferry

FOR MY journey ahead Grandmother had parted me a red packet, inside of which was dollar. This being an old custom and old people always do this when the young leave home.

Susan too had a gift.

She said she would go with me on the ferry and all the way to the airport. This I liked very much and so did Grandmother. It's the sort of thing a big sister would do.

The ferry was late and there was plenty of time for me to tell Susan about my last dream.

"It was a girl," I said.

"What was she like?"

"She was blonde," I replied, blonde and golden as the sun glittering across the waves I was about to say but Grandmother who was sat behind us said, Careful you two! Don't fall into the sea!

"She was tall. Like you. But blonde. Golden hair and long."

"And?"

"She comes on the ferry. She comes to Joan Island. She will come today. That's all I remember."

The funny thing is, when the ferry did come there was a blonde. I was looking at her as she passed me by and because of this, I tripped and fell to my knees. The next thing I knew someone was picking me up. I thought it might have been Susan but it was not.

"Are you alright?"

She had blues eyes and long, golden hair. A big pack was on her back. I did not say anything. The ferry was honking. People were late. I slowly nodded and moved on. The ferry soon left the island.

"She come to see you go," Susan said, meaning Wando. "This was her life and work before the station closed. Every day she come to see people both to go and return. She is happy now. She knows you will return."

I said nothing and continued to look at the pier till Wando and Grandmother was out of sight.

"*Basmatu minchun?*" I asked, which means: What will you do when I am gone?

Susan looked up from what she was reading and smiled, saying, "I will go and water the garden."

"You won't get married?"

"No," she said and smiled once more. "And you? What will you do?"

I looked away and slowly raised my eyebrow as if to say I haven't the foggiest.

I switched off my radio. I got up and went to lean over the window. A cool breeze was blowing.

The last thing I saw of the island was my auntie's bell tower. It was like a head sticking up out of the trees and looking across the sea.

I thought of Wando. And how she would have quickly returned back up the hill to the station and perhaps sit with the cat. But mostly I thought of the stranger.

I thought about her golden locks and sky blue dress standing outside the locked gate beginning to unlock the gate with a key. A key the gate and the station had not seen for a long, long time.

Author's Note

Joan Island is based on Long Island or Cheung Chau. This place south of Hong Kong is where my Grandfather once ran a temple retreat. It was a small and humble building set high up in the hills overlooking the sea. In some ways it was like a hostel, but of the spirit.

I was about three years old the first time I stayed over. And yet despite a brain made of straw I could remember how high in the sky the place was, the sound of the sea, the shade from the trees, breakfast and, a funny two finned plane that flew high above us. I did not go back until decades later when memories of the place resurfaced (perhaps because I needed it) but by then it was closed and left to ruin.

The last people to see the retreat open were two sisters: my aunty and my mother. It is they who told me about the resident dog that walked pilgrims down to the water front and onto the ferry going home.

This book Midnight Train To Joan is homage to this splendid animal and place and also the films I saw while I was away at college which are the times I was most happy. Alice In The Cities (1973), The Day of The Triffids (1962) and the wonderful Sommarlek (1951). In writing I am grateful to the works of Zoe Lucas, Emilia Hazelip, Jack Hargreaves, Martin Crawford, Sheila Hirtle, Wayne H. McAlister to whom I quote: "You begin to feel...as if somehow you've always been here and never anywhere else", my tutors Dave Brodie and Jon Cook, and especially to Yella as Alice and Janina as Susan for they are the true source of this spring. Perhaps this is the reason why Midnight Train To Joan is in part a picture book. A picture about a dog who knew The Way snapped among the bright summer days of travel.

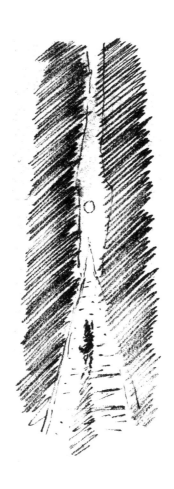

Vivian Truong

Po Wah Lam is really a girls' name but he is happy with this because he likes them and anything that lives on the earth and off it. After studying interior design he became the first winner of the David Wong Writing Fellowship at the University of East Anglia, England. He left the Far East at a young age but for a long time kept dreaming a running dog welcome his return. This *beckoning* is the basis for his storytelling. Thank you for reading and dreaming!

https://midnighttraintojoan.wordpress.com/

26495247R00131

Printed in Great Britain
by Amazon